PUFFIN CLASSICS

Rip van Winkle

Washington Irving (1783–1859) was born into a well-to-do family in New York, the youngest of eleven children, and was named after the great future president, George Washington.

Young Washington had a patchy education, but developed an early passion for books and writing. As an adult, he was lucky enough not to have to worry about making a living, since the family's import-export business was thriving. Irving practised law for a few years, but he preferred writing occasional pieces for newspapers and magazines.

His first book, *Knickerbocker's History of New York* (1809), was the earliest American humorous book which could also be called literature. Despite its great success, however, Irving remained only a part-time writer. In 1815 he moved to Liverpool, to manage the British end of the family business for a year or two. He ended up staying in Europe for seventeen years.

The family business collapsed in 1817 and Irving suddenly found that he had to make a living. The fame of *Knickerbocker's History* had enabled him to meet and become friendly with leading British literary figures, and they encouraged him to take up serious writing. The immediate result was the book on which Irving's lasting fame depends – *The Sketch Book of Geoffrey Crayon, Gent.* (1819–20). Among the portraits of British life in this book, Irving included his two most famous fantasy stories, 'Rip van Winkle' and 'The Legend of Sleepy Hollow'. This Puffin edition contains these two stories and others, which came from later collections of essays and stories.

He continued to write for some years, but increasingly concentrated on a diplomatic career; in particular, he spent two periods as an ambassador in Spain. Out of this came his *Life of Columbus*, which is recognized as the first American history book. Irving's title as the 'father of American literature' is due not just to his charming and lucid style of writing, but also to the fact that he was breaking new ground. Many other great American writers were to follow, but he was the first.

Some other Puffin Classics to enjoy

THE HAPPY PRINCE AND OTHER STORIES
Oscar Wilde

JUST SO STORIES
Rudyard Kipling

PETER PAN
J. M. Barrie

THE WIZARD OF OZ
L. Frank Baum

WASHINGTON IRVING

Rip van Winkle
and other stories

PUFFIN BOOKS

PUFFIN BOOKS

Published by the Penguin Group
Penguin Books Ltd, 27 Wrights Lane, London W8 5TZ, England
Penguin Books USA Inc., 375 Hudson Street, New York, New York 10014, USA
Penguin Books Australia Ltd, Ringwood, Victoria, Australia
Penguin Books Canada Ltd, 10 Alcorn Avenue, Toronto, Ontario, Canada M4V 3B2
Penguin Books (NZ) Ltd, 182–190 Wairau Road, Auckland 10, New Zealand

Penguin Books Ltd, Registered Offices: Harmondsworth, Middlesex, England

First published 1905
Published in Puffin Books 1986
Reissued in this edition 1994
3 5 7 9 10 8 6 4 2

Filmset by Datix International Limited, Bungay, Suffolk
Printed in England by Clays Ltd, St Ives plc
Set in 12/15 pt Monophoto Plantin

CONTENTS

Rip Van Winkle

POSTHUMOUS WRITING OF
DIEDRICH KNICKERBOCKER

By Woden, God of Saxons,
From whence comes Wensday, that is
    Wodensday,
Truth is a thing that ever I will keep
Unto thylke day in which I creep into
My sepulchre –

CARTWRIGHT

[The following Tale was found among the papers of the late Diedrich Knickerbocker, an old gentleman of New York, who was very curious in the Dutch history of the province and the manners of the descendants from its primitive settlers. His historical researches, however, did not lie so much among books as among men, for the former are lamentably scanty on his favourite topics, whereas he found the old burghers, and still more their wives, rich in that legendary lore so invaluable to true history. Whenever, therefore, he happened upon a genuine Dutch family, snugly shut up in its low-roofed farm-house, under a spreading syca-more, he looked upon it as a little clasped volume of black letter and studied it with the zeal of a bookworm.

The result of all these researches was a history of the province during the reign of the Dutch governors, which he published some years since. There have been various opinions as to the literary character of his work, and, to tell the truth, it is not a whit better than it should be. Its chief merit is its scrupulous accuracy, which indeed was a little questioned on its first appearance, but has since been completely established, and it is now admitted into all historical collections as a book of unquestionable authority.

The old gentleman died shortly after the publica-tion of his work, and now that he is dead and gone, it cannot do much harm to his memory to say that his time might have been much better employed in weightier labours. He, however, was apt to ride his hobby his own way; and though it did now and then kick up the dust a little in the eyes of his neighbours and grieve the spirit of some friends, for whom he felt the truest deference and affection, yet his errors and follies are remem-bered 'more in sorrow than in anger', and it begins to be suspected that he never intended to injure or offend. But however his memory may be appreci-ated by critics, it is still held dear by many folks, whose good opinion is well worth having; particu-larly by certain biscuit bakers, who have gone so far as to imprint his likeness on their new-year cakes, and have thus given him a chance for immortality, almost equal to being stamped on a Waterloo Medal, or a Queen Anne's Farthing.]

Whoever has made a voyage up the Hudson must remember the Kaatskill Mountains. They are a dismembered branch of the great Appalachian family, and are seen away to the west of the river, swelling up to a noble height and lording it over the surrounding country. Every change of season, every change of weather, indeed, every hour of the day produces some change in the magical hues and shapes of these mountains, and they are regarded by all the good wives, far and near, as perfect barometers. When the weather is fair and settled, they are clothed in blue and purple, and print their bold outlines on the clear evening sky but, sometimes, when the rest of the landscape is cloudless, they will gather a hood of grey vapours about their summits, which, in the last rays of the setting sun, will glow and light up like a crown of glory.

At the foot of these fairy mountains, the voyager may have described the light smoke curling up from a village, whose shingle roofs gleam among the trees, just where the blue tints of the upland melt away into the fresh green of the nearer landscape. It is a little village of great antiquity, having been founded by some of the Dutch colonists in the early times of the province, just about the beginning of the government of the good Peter Stuyvesant (may he rest in peace!), and there were some of the houses of the original settlers standing within a few years, built of small yellow bricks brought from Holland, having latticed windows and gable fronts, surmounted with weathercocks.

In that same village, and in one of these very houses (which, to tell the precise truth, was sadly time-worn and weather-beaten), there lived many years since, while the country was yet a province of Great Britain, a simple, good-natured fellow of the name of Rip Van Winkle. He was a descendant of the Van Winkles who figured so gallantly in the chivalrous days of Peter Stuyvesant, and accompanied him to the siege of Fort Christina. He inherited, however, but little of the martial character of his ancestors. I have observed that he was a simple, good-natured man; he was, moreover, a kind neighbour, and an obedient, henpecked husband. Indeed, to the latter circumstance might be owing that meekness of spirit which gained him such universal popularity, for those men are most apt to be obsequious and conciliating abroad who are under the discipline of shrews at home. Their tempers, doubtless, are rendered pliant and malleable in the fiery furnace of domestic tribulation, and a curtain lecture is worth all the sermons in the world for teaching the virtues of patience and long-suffering. A termagant wife may, therefore, in some respects, be considered a tolerable blessing and if so, Rip Van Winkle was thrice blessed.

Certain it is that he was a great favourite among all the good wives of the village, who, as usual with the amiable sex, took his part in all family squabbles and never failed, whenever they talked those matters over in their evening gossipings, to lay all the blame on Dame Van Winkle. The children of the, village, too, would shout with joy whenever he approached. He assisted at their sports, made their playthings, taught them to fly kites and shoot marbles, and told them long stories of ghosts, witches, and Indians. Whenever he went dodging about the village, he was surrounded by a troop of them, hanging on his skirts, clambering on his back, and playing a thousand tricks on him with impunity; and not a dog would bark at him throughout the neighbourhood.

The great error in Rip's composition was an insuperable aversion to all kinds of profitable labour. It could not be from the want of assiduity or perseverance, for he would sit on a wet rock, with a rod as long and heavy as a Tartar's lance, and fish all day without a murmur, even though he should not be encouraged by a single nibble. He would carry a fowling piece on his shoulder for hours together, trudging through woods and swamps and up hill and down dale to shoot a few squirrels or wild pigeons. He would never refuse to assist a neighbour even in the roughest toil, and was a foremost man at all country frolics for husking Indian corn or building stone fences; the women of the village, too, used to employ him to run their errands and to do such little odd jobs as their less obliging husbands would not do for them. In a word, Rip was ready to attend to anybody's business but his own; but as to doing family duty and keeping his farm in order, he found it impossible.

In fact, he declared it was of no use to work on his farm; it was the most pestilent little piece of ground in the whole country; everything about it went wrong, and would go wrong, in spite of him. His fences were continually falling to pieces; his cow would either go astray or get among the cabbages; weeds were sure to grow quicker in his fields than anywhere else; the rain always made a point of setting in just as he had some outdoor work to do; so that though his patrimonial estate had dwindled away under his management, acre by acre, until there was little more left than a mere patch of Indian corn and potatoes, yet it was the worst-conditioned farm in the neighbour-hood.

His children, too, were as ragged and wild as if they belonged to nobody. His son Rip, an urchin begotten in his own likeness, promised to inherit the habits, with the old clothes, of his father. He was generally seen trooping like a colt at his mother's heels, equipped in a pair of his father's cast-off galligaskins, which he had much ado to hold up with one hand as a fine lady does her train in bad weather.

Rip Van Winkle, however, was one of those

happy mortals of foolish, well-oiled dispositions
who take the world easy, eat white bread or brown,
whichever can be got with least thought or trouble,
and would rather starve on a penny than work for
a pound. If left to himself, he would have whistled
life away in perfect contentment but his wife kept
continually dinning in his ears about his idleness,
his carelessness, and the ruin he was bringing on
his family. Morning, noon, and night, her tongue
was incessantly going, and everything he said or
did was sure to produce a torrent of household
eloquence. Rip had but one way of replying to all
lectures of the kind, and that, by frequent use,
had grown into a habit. He shrugged his shoulders, shook his head, cast up his eyes, but said
nothing. This, however, always provoked a fresh
volley from his wife, so that he was fain to draw
off his forces and take to the outside of the house
– the only side which, in truth, belongs to a
henpecked husband.

Rip's sole domestic adherent was his dog, Wolf,
who was as much henpecked as his master, for
Dame Van Winkle regarded them as companions
in idleness, and even looked upon Wolf with an
evil eye as the cause of his master's going so often
astray. True it is, in all points of spirit befitting
an honourable dog, he was as courageous an
animal as ever scoured the woods – but what
courage can withstand the ever-during and all-be-
setting terrors of a woman's tongue? The moment
Wolf entered the house his crest fell, his tail

drooped to the ground, or curled between his legs, he sneaked about with a gallows air, casting many a sidelong glance at Dame Van Winkle, and at the least flourish of a broomstick or ladle he would fly to the door with yelping precipitation.

Times grew worse and worse with Rip Van Winkle as years of matrimony rolled on; a tart temper never mellows with age, and a shad tongue is the only edged tool that grows keener with constant use. For a long while he used to console himself, when driven from home, by frequenting a kind of perpetual club of the sages, philosophers, and other idle personages of the village, which held its sessions on a bench before a small inn, designated by a rubicund portrait of His Majesty George the Third. Here they used to sit in the shade through a long, lazy summer's day, talking listlessly over village gossip or telling endless sleepy stories about nothing. But it would have been worth any statesman's money to have heard the profound discussions that sometimes took place when by chance an old newspaper fell into their hands from some passing traveller. How solemnly they would listen to the contents, as drawled out by Derrick Van Bummel, the school-master, a dapper, learned little man who was not to be daunted by the most gigantic word in the dictionary; and how sagely they would deliberate upon public events some months after they had taken place.

The opinions of this junto were completely

controlled by Nicholas Vedder, a patriarch of the village and land-lord of the inn, at the door of which he took his seat from morning till night, just moving sufficiently to avoid the sun and keep in the shade of a large tree, so that the neighbours could tell the hour by his movements as accurately as by a sundial. It is true he was rarely heard to speak, but smoked his pipe incessantly. His adherents, however (for every great man has his adherents), perfectly understood him, and knew how to gather his opinions. When anything that was read or related displeased him, he was observed to smoke his pipe vehemently and to send forth short, frequent, and angry puffs; but when pleased, he would inhale the smoke slowly and tranquilly and emit it in light and placid clouds, and sometimes, taking the pipe from his mouth and letting the fragrant vapour curl about his nose, would gravely nod his head in token of perfect approbation.

From even this stronghold the unlucky Rip was at length routed by his termagant wife, who would suddenly break in upon the tranquillity of the assemblage and call the members all to naught; nor was that august personage, Nicholas Vedder himself, sacred from the daring tongue of this terrible virago, who charged him outright with encouraging her husband in habits of idleness.

Poor Rip was at last reduced almost to despair, and his only alternative, to escape from the labour of the farm and clamour of his wife, was to take gun in hand and stroll away into the woods. Here he would sometimes seat himself at the foot of a tree and share the contents of his wallet with Wolf, with whom he sympathized as a fellow sufferer in persecution. 'Poor Wolf,' he would say, 'thy mistress leads thee a dog's life of it; but never mind, my lad, whilst I live thou shalt never want a friend to stand by thee!' Wolf would wag his tail, look wistfully in his master's face, and if dogs can feel pity, I verily believe he reciprocated the sentiment with all his heart.

In a long ramble of the kind of a fine autumnal day, Rip had unconsciously scrambled to one of the highest parts of the Kaatskill Mountains. He was after his favourite sport of squirrel shooting, and the still solitudes had echoed and re-echoed with the reports of his gun. Panting and fatigued, he threw himself, late in the afternoon, on a green knoll, covered with mountain herbage, that crowned the brow of a precipice. From an opening between the trees he could overlook all the lower country for many a mile of rich woodland. He saw at a distance the lordly Hudson, far, far below him, moving on its silent but majestic course, with the reflection of a purple cloud or the sail of a lagging bark here and there sleeping on its glassy bosom, and at last losing itself in the blue highlands.

On the other side he looked down into a deep mountain glen, wild, lonely, and shagged, the bottom filled with fragments from the impending cliffs, and scarcely lighted by the reflected rays of the setting sun. For some time Rip lay musing on this scene. Evening was gradually advancing; the mountains began to throw their long blue shadows over the valleys. He saw that it would be dark long before he could reach the village, and he heaved a heavy sigh when he thought of encountering the terrors of Dame Van Winkle.

As he was about to descend, he heard a voice from a distance, hallooing, 'Rip Van Winkle! Rip Van Winkle!' He looked around, but could see nothing but a crow winging its solitary flight across the mountain. He thought his fancy must have deceived him, and turned again to descend, when he heard the same cry ring through the still evening air, 'Rip Van Winkle! Rip Van Winkle!' At the same time Wolf bristled up his back and, giving a low growl, skulked to his master's side, looking fearfully down into the glen. Rip now felt a vague apprehension stealing over him; he looked anxiously in the same direction and perceived a strange figure slowly toiling up the rocks, and bending under the weight of something he carried on his back. He was surprised to see any human being in this lonely and unfrequented place, but supposing it to be some one of the neighbourhood in need of his assistance, he hastened down to yield it.

On nearer approach he was still more surprised at the singularity of the stranger's appearance. He was a short, square-built old fellow, with thick, bushy hair and a grizzled beard. His dress was of the antique Dutch fashion – a cloth jerkin strapped around the waist and several pairs of breeches, the outer one of ample volume, decorated with rows of buttons down the sides and bunches at the knees. He bore on his shoulder a stout keg that seemed full of liquor, and made signs for Rip to approach and assist him with the load. Though rather shy and distrustful of this new acquaintance, Rip complied with his usual alacrity, and mutually relieving one another, they clambered up a narrow gully, apparently the dry bed of a mountain torrent. As they ascended, Rip every now and then heard long rolling peals, like distant thunder, that seemed to issue out of a deep ravine, or rather cleft, between lofty rocks, toward which their rugged path conducted. He paused for an instant, but supposing it to be the muttering of one of those transient thunder showers which often take place in mountain heights, he proceeded. Passing through the ravine, they came to a hollow, like a small amphitheatre, surrounded by perpendicular precipices, over the brinks of which impending trees shot their branches, so that you only caught glimpses of the azure sky and the bright evening cloud. During the whole time, Rip and his companion had laboured on in silence, for though the former marvelled greatly what could be the object of carrying a keg of liquor up this wild mountain, yet there was something strange and incomprehensible about the unknown that inspired awe and checked familiarity.

On entering the amphitheatre, new objects of wonder were to be seen. On a level spot in the centre was a company of odd-looking personages playing at ninepins. They were dressed in a quaint, outlandish fashion; some wore short doublets, others jerkins, with long knives in their belts, and most of them had enormous breeches, of similar style with that of the guide's. Their visages, too, were peculiar; one had a large beard, broad face, and small piggish eyes, the face of another seemed to consist entirely of nose and was surmounted by a white sugar-loaf hat set off with a little red cock's tail. They all had beards, of various shapes and colours. There was one who seemed to be the commander. He was a stout old gentleman, with a weather-beaten countenance; he wore a laced doublet, broad belt and hanger, high-crowned hat and feather, red stockings, and high-heeled shoes, with roses in them. The whole group reminded Rip of the figures in an old Flemish painting, in the parlour of Dominie Van Shaick, the village parson, and which had been brought over from Holland at the time of the settlement.

What seemed particularly odd to Rip was that though these folks were evidently amusing themselves, yet they maintained the gravest faces, the most mysterious silence, and were, withal, the most melancholy party of pleasure he had ever witnessed. Nothing interrupted the stillness of the scene but the noise of the balls, which, whenever they were rolled, echoed along the mountains like rumbling peals of thunder.

As Rip and his companion approached them, they suddenly desisted from their play and stared at him with such fixed, statuelike gaze and such strange, uncouth, lacklustre countenances that his heart turned within him and his knees smote together. His companion now emptied the contents of the keg into large flagons and made signs to him to wait upon the company. He obeyed with fear and trembling; they quaffed the liquor in profound silence and then returned to their game.

By degrees Rip's awe and apprehension subsided. He even ventured, when no eye was fixed upon him, to taste the beverage, which he found had much of the flavour of excellent Hollands. He was naturally a thirsty soul and was soon tempted to repeat the draught. One taste provoked another; and he reiterated his visits to the flagon so often that at length his senses were overpowered, his eyes swam in his head, his head gradually declined, and he fell into a deep sleep.

On waking, he found himself on the green knoll whence he had first seen the old man of the glen. He rubbed his eyes – it was a bright, sunny morning. The birds were hopping and twittering among the bushes, and the eagle was wheeling aloft and breasting the pure mountain breeze.

'Surely,' thought Rip, 'I have not slept here all night.' He recalled the occurrences before he fell asleep. The strange man with a keg of liquor – the mountain ravine – the wild retreat among the rocks – the woebegone party at ninepins – the flagon – 'Oh! That flagon! That wicked flagon!' thought Rip. 'What excuse shall I make to Dame Van Winkle?'

He looked around for his gun, but in place of the clean, well-oiled fowling piece he found an old firelock lying by him, the barrel encrusted with rust, the lock falling off, and the stock worm-eaten. He now suspected that the grave roysters of the mountain had put a trick upon him, and, having dosed him with liquor, had robbed him of his gun. Wolf, too, had disappeared, but he might have strayed away after a squirrel or partridge. He whistled after him and shouted his name, but all in vain; the echoes repeated his whistle and shout, but no dog was to be seen.

He determined to revisit the scene of the last evening's gambol, and if he met with any of the party, to demand his dog and gun. As he rose to walk, he found himself stiff in the joints and wanting in his usual activity. 'These mountain beds do not agree with me,' thought Rip, 'and if this frolic should lay me up with a fit of the rheumatism, I shall have a blessed time with Dame Van Winkle.' With some difficulty he got down into the glen; he found the gully up which he and his companion had ascended the preceding evening, but to his astonishment a mountain stream was now foaming down it, leaping from rock to rock and filling the glen with babbling murmurs. He, however, made shift to scramble up its sides, working his toilsome way through thickets of birch, sassafras, and witch hazel, and sometimes tripped up or entangled by the wild grapevines that twisted their coils or tendrils from tree to tree and spread a kind of network in his path.

At length he reached to where the ravine had opened through the cliffs to the amphitheatre, but no traces of such opening remained. The rocks presented a high, impenetrable wall over which the torrent came tumbling in a sheet of feathery foam and fell into a broad, deep basin, black from the shadows of the surrounding forest. Here, then, poor Rip was brought to a stand. He again called and whistled after his dog; he was only answered by the cawing of a flock of idle crows, sporting high in air about a dry tree that overhung a sunny precipice, and who, secure in their elevation, seemed to look down and scoff at the poor man's perplexities. What was to be done? The morning was passing away, and Rip felt famished for want of his breakfast. He grieved to give up his dog and gun he dreaded to meet his wife, but it would not do to starve among the mountains. He shook his head, shouldered the rusty firelock, and, with a heart full of trouble and anxiety, turned his steps homeward.

As he approached the village he met a number

of people, but none whom he knew, which somewhat surprised him, for he had thought himself acquainted with every one in the country around. Their dress, too, was of a different fashion from that to which he was accustomed. They all stared at him with equal marks of surprise, and whenever they cast their eyes upon him invariably stroked their chins. The constant recurrence of this gesture induced Rip, involuntarily, to do the same, when, to his astonishment, he found his beard had grown a foot long!

He had now entered the skirts of the village. A troop of strange children ran at his heels, hooting after him and pointing at his grey beard. The dogs, too, not one of which he recognized for an old acquaintance, barked at him as he passed. The very village was altered; it was larger and more populous. There were rows of houses which he had never seen before, and those which had been his familiar haunts had disappeared. Strange names were over the doors – strange faces at the windows – everything was strange. His mind now misgave him; he began to doubt whether both he and the world around him were not bewitched. Surely this was his native village, which he had left but the day before. There stood the Kaatskill Mountains – there ran the silver Hudson at a distance – there was every hill and dale precisely as it had always been. Rip was sorely perplexed. 'That flagon last night,' thought he, 'has addled my poor head sadly!'

It was with some difficulty that he found the way to his own house, which he approached with silent awe, expecting every moment to hear the shrill voice of Dame Van Winkle. He found the house gone to decay – the roof fallen in, the windows shattered, and the doors off the hinges. A half-starved dog that looked like Wolf was skulking about it. Rip called him by name, but the cur snarled, showed his teeth, and passed on. This was an unkind cut indeed. 'My very dog,' sighed poor Rip, 'has forgotten me!'

He entered the house, which, to tell the truth, Dame Van Winkle had always kept in neat order. It was empty, forlorn, and apparently abandoned. This desolateness overcame all his connubial fears – he called loudly for his wife and children; the lonely chambers rang for a moment with his voice, and then all again was silence.

He now hurried forth and hastened to his old resort, the village inn – but it too was gone. A large, rickety, wooden building stood in its place, with great gaping windows, some of them broken and mended with old hats and petticoats, and over the door was painted, 'the Union Hotel, by Jonathan Doolittle'. Instead of the great tree that used to shelter the quiet little Dutch inn of yore, there now was reared a tall, naked pole, with something on the top that looked like a red nightcap, and from it was fluttering a flag, on which was a singular assemblage of stars and stripes – all this was strange and incomprehensible. He recognized on the sign, however, the ruby face of King George, under which he had smoked so many a peaceful pipe; but even this was singularly metamorphosed. The red coat was changed for one of blue and buff, a sword was held in the hand instead of a sceptre, the head was decorated with a cocked hat, and underneath was painted in large characters, GENERAL WASHINGTON.

There was, as usual, a crowd of folk about the door, but none that Rip recollected. The very character of the people seemed changed. There was a busy, bustling, disputatious tone about it, instead of the accustomed phlegm and drowsy tranquillity. He looked in vain for the sage Nicholas Vedder, with his broad face, double chin, and fair long pipe, uttering clouds of tobacco smoke instead of idle speeches; or Van Bummel, the schoolmaster, doling forth the contents of an ancient newspaper. In place of these, a lean, bilious-looking fellow, with his pockets full of handbills, was haranguing vehemently about rights of citizens – elections – members of congress – liberty – Bunker's Hill – heroes of Seventy-six – and other words, which were a perfect Babylonish jargon to the bewildered Van Winkle.

The appearance of Rip, with his long, grizzled beard, his rusty fowling piece, his uncouth dress, and an army of women and children at his heels, soon attracted the attention of the tavern politicians. They crowded around him, eyeing him from head to foot with great curiosity. The orator bustled up to him and, drawing him partly aside, inquired 'on which side he voted?' Rip stared in vacant stupidity. Another short but busy little fellow pulled him by the arm, and, rising on tiptoe, inquired in his ear, 'whether he was Federal or Democrat?' Rip was equally at a loss to comprehend the question; when a knowing, self-important old gentleman in a sharp cocked hat made his way through the crowd, putting them to the right and left with his elbows as he passed, and, planting himself before Van Winkle, with one arm akimbo, the other resting on his cane, his keen eyes and sharp hat penetrating, as it were, into his very soul, demanded in an austere tone, 'what brought him to the election with a gun on his shoulder, and a mob at his heels, and whether he meant to breed a riot in the village?' 'Alas! Gentlemen,' cried Rip, somewhat dismayed, 'I am a poor, quiet man, a native of the place, and a loyal subject of the king, God bless him!'

Here a general shout burst from the bystanders. 'A tory! A tory! A spy! A refugee! Hustle him! Away with him!' It was with great difficulty that the self-important man in the cocked hat restored order; and, having assumed a tenfold austerity of brow, demanded again of the unknown culprit what he came there for and whom he was seeking. The poor man humbly assured him that he meant no harm, but merely came there in search of some of his neighbours, who used to keep about the tavern.

'Well – who are they? Name them.'

Rip bethought himself a moment, and inquired, 'Where's Nicholas Vedder?'

There was a silence for a little while, when an old man replied, in a thin, piping voice, 'Nicholas Vedder! Why, he is dead and gone these eighteen years! There was a wooden tombstone in the churchyard that used to tell about him, but that's rotten and gone too.'

'Where's Brom Dutcher?'

'Oh, he went off to the army in the beginning of the war; some say he was killed at the storming of Stony Point – others say he was drowned in a squall at the foot of Antony's Nose. I don't know – he never came back again.'

'Where's Van Bummel, the schoolmaster?'

'He went off to the wars, too, was a great militia general, and is now in congress.'

Rip's heart died away at hearing of these sad changes in his home and friends, and finding himself thus alone in the world. Every answer puzzled him, too, by treating of such enormous lapses of time and of matters which he could not understand: war – congress – Stony Point. He had no courage to ask after any more friends, but cried out in despair, 'Does nobody here know Rip Van Winkle?'

'Oh, Rip Van Winkle!' exclaimed two or three. 'Oh, to be sure! That's Rip Van Winkle yonder, leaning against the tree.'

Rip looked, and beheld a precise counterpart of

himself as he went up the mountain: apparently as lazy, and certainly as ragged. The poor fellow was now completely confounded. He doubted his own identity, and whether he was himself or another man. In the midst of his bewilderment, the man in the cocked hat demanded who he was, and what was his name?

'God knows,' exclaimed he, at his wit's end. 'I'm not myself – I'm somebody else – that's me yonder – no – that's somebody else got into my shoes – I was myself last night, but I fell asleep on the mountain, and they've changed my gun, and everything's changed, and I'm changed, and I can't tell what's my name, or who I am!'

The bystanders began now to look at each other, nod, wink significantly, and tap their fingers against their foreheads. There was a whisper also about securing the gun and keeping the old fellow from doing mischief, at the very suggestion of which the self-important man in the cocked hat retired with some precipitation. At this critical moment a fresh, comely woman pressed through the throng to get a peep at the grey-bearded man. She had a chubby child in her arms, which, frightened at his looks, began to cry. 'Hush, Rip,' cried she, 'hush, you little fool; the old man won't hurt you.' The name of the child, the air of the mother, the tone of her voice, all awakened a train of recollections in his mind. 'What is your name, my good woman?' asked he.

'Judith Gardenier.'

'And your father's name?'

'Ah, poor man, Rip Van Winkle was his name, but it's twenty years since he went away from home with his gun, and never has been heard of since – his dog came home without him; but whether he shot himself, or was carried away by the Indians, nobody can tell. I was then but a little girl.'

Rip had but one question more to ask; but he put it with a faltering voice:

'Where's your mother?'

'Oh, she too had died but a short time since; she broke a blood vessel in a fit of passion, at a New England pedlar.'

There was a drop of comfort, at least, in this intelligence. The honest man could contain himself no longer. He caught his daughter and her child in his arms. 'I am your father!' cried he. 'Young Rip Van Winkle once – old Rip Van Winkle now! Does nobody know poor Rip Van Winkle?'

All stood amazed, until an old woman, tottering out from among the crowd, put her hand to her brow and, peering under it in his face for a moment, exclaimed, 'Sure enough! It is Rip Van Winkle – it is himself! Welcome home again, old neighbour. Why, where have you been these twenty long years?'

Rip's story was soon told, for the whole twenty years had been to him but as one night. The neighbours stared when they heard it; some were seen to wink at each other and put their tongues in their cheeks, and the self-important man in the cocked hat, who, when the alarm was over, had returned to the field, screwed down the corners of his mouth and shook his head – upon which there was a general shaking of the head throughout the assemblage.

It was determined, however, to take the opinion of old Peter Vanderdonk, who was seen slowly advancing up the road. He was a descendant of the historian of that name, who wrote one of the earliest accounts of the province. Peter was the most ancient inhabitant of the village, and well versed in all the wonderful events and traditions of the neighbourhood. He recollected Rip at once and corroborated his story in the most satisfactory manner. He assured the company that it was a fact, handed down from his ancestor the historian, that the Kaatskill Mountains had always been haunted by strange beings. That it was affirmed that the great Hendrick Hudson, the first discoverer of the river and country, kept a kind of vigil there every twenty years, with his crew of the *Half Moon*, being permitted in this way to revisit the scenes of his enterprise and keep a guardian eye upon the river and the great city called by his name. That his father had once seen them in their old Dutch dresses playing at ninepins in a hollow of the mountain, and that he himself had heard, one summer afternoon, the sound of their balls, like distant peals of thunder.

To make a long story short, the company broke up and returned to the more important concerns of the election. Rip's daughter took him home to live with her; she had a snug, well-furnished house, and a stout, cheery farmer for a husband, whom Rip recollected for one of the urchins that used to climb upon his back. As to Rip's son, and heir, who was the ditto of himself, seen leaning against the tree, he was employed to work on the farm, but evinced a hereditary disposition to attend to anything else but his business.

Rip now resumed his old walk and habits; he soon found many of his former cronies, though all rather the worse for the wear and tear of time, and preferred making friends among the rising generation, with whom he soon grew into great favour.

Having nothing to do at home, and being arrived at that happy age when a man can be idle with impunity, he took his place once more on the bench at the inn door and was reverenced as one of the patriarchs of the village, and a chronicle of the old times 'before the war'. It was some time before he could get into the regular track of gossip, or could be made to comprehend the strange events that had taken place during his torpor. How that there had been a revolutionary war – that the country had thrown off the yoke of old England – and that, instead of being a subject of his Majesty George the Third, he was now a free citizen of the United States. Rip, in fact, was no politician – the changes of states and empires made but little impression on him; but there was one species of despotism under which he had long groaned, and that was – petticoat government. Happily that was at an end; he had got his neck out of the yoke of matrimony and could go in and out whenever he pleased, without dreading the tyranny of Dame Van Winkle. Whenever her name was mentioned, however, he shook his head, shrugged his shoulders, and cast up his eyes, which might pass either for an expression of resignation to his fate or joy at his deliverance.

He used to tell his story to every stranger that arrived at Mr Doolittle's hotel. He was observed, at first, to vary on some points every time he told it, which was, doubtless, owing to his having so recently awaked. It at last settled down precisely to the tale I have related, and not a man, woman, or child in the neighbourhood but knew it by heart. Some always pretended to doubt the reality of it, and insisted that Rip had been out of his head, and that this was one point on which he always remained flighty. The old Dutch inhabitants, however, almost universally gave it full credit. Even to this day they never hear a thunderstorm of a summer afternoon about the Kaatskill but they say Hendrick Hudson and his crew are at their game of ninepins; and it is a common wish of all henpecked husbands in the neighbourhood, when life hangs heavy on their hands, that they might have a quieting draught out of Rip Van Winkle's flagon.

NOTE

The foregoing Tale, one would suspect, had been suggested to Mr Knickerbocker by a little German superstition about the Emperor Frederick *der Roth-bart* and the Kypphaüser mountain. The subjoined note, however, which he had appended to the tale, shows that it is an absolute fact, narrated with his usual fidelity:

'The story of Rip Van Winkle may seem incredible to many, but nevertheless I give it my full belief, for I know the vicinity of our old Dutch settlements to have been very subject to marvellous events and appearances. Indeed, I have heard many stranger stories than this, in the villages along the Hudson, all of which were too well authenticated to admit of a doubt. I have even talked with Rip Van Winkle myself, who, when last I saw him, was a very venerable old man and so perfectly rational and consistent on every other point that I think no conscientious person could refuse to take this into the bargain; nay, I have seen a certificate on the subject taken before a country justice and signed with a cross, in the justice's own handwriting. The story, therefore, is beyond the possibility of doubt.

D. K.'

POSTSCRIPT

The following are travelling notes from a memorandum book of Mr Knickerbocker:

The Kaatsberg, or Catskill Mountains, have always been a region full of fable. The Indians considered them the abode of spirits who influenced the weather, spreading sunshine or clouds over the landscape, and sending good or bad hunting seasons. They were ruled by an old squaw spirit, said to be their mother. She dwelt on the highest peak of the Catskills and had charge of the doors of day and night, to open and shut them at the proper hour. She hung up the new moons in the skies and cut up the old ones into stars. In times of drought, if properly propitiated, she would spin light summer clouds out of cobwebs and morning dew and send them off from the crest of the mountain, flake after flake, like flakes of carded cotton, to float in the air; until, dissolved by the heat of the sun, they would fall in gentle showers, causing the grass to spring, the fruits to ripen, and the corn to grow an inch an hour. If displeased, however, she would brew up clouds black as ink, sitting in the midst of them like a bottle-bellied spider in the midst of its web; and when these clouds broke, woe betide the valleys!

In old times, say the Indian traditions, there was a kind of Manitou or Spirit, who kept about the wildest recesses of the Catskill Mountains, and took a mischievous pleasure in wreaking all kinds of evils and vexations upon the red men. Sometimes he would assume the form of a bear, a panther, or a deer, lead the bewildered hunter a weary chase through tangled forests and among ragged rocks, and then spring off with a loud ho! ho! leaving him aghast on the brink of a beetling precipice or raging torrent.

The favourite abode of this Manitou is still shown. It is a great rock or cliff on the loneliest part of the mountains, and, from the flowering vines which clamber about it and the wild flowers which abound in its neighbourhood, is known by the name of the Garden Rock. Near the foot of it is a small lake, the haunt of the solitary bittern, with water snakes basking in the sun on the leaves of the pond lilies which lie on the surface. This place was held in great awe by the Indians, insomuch that the boldest hunter would not pursue his game within its precincts. Once upon a time, however, a hunter who had lost his way penetrated to the Garden Rock, where he beheld a number of gourds placed in the crotches of trees. One of these he seized and made off with, but in the hurry of his retreat he let it fall among the rocks, when a great stream gushed forth, which washed him away and swept him down precipices, where he was dashed to pieces, and the stream made its way to the Hudson and continues to flow to the present day; being the identical stream known by the name of the Kaaters-kill.

THE LEGEND OF SLEEPY HOLLOW

FOUND AMONG THE PAPERS OF
THE LATE DIEDRICH KNICKERBOCKER

A pleasing land of drowsy head it was,
   Of dreams that wave before the half-shut eye;
And of gay castles in the clouds that pass,
   For ever flushing round a summer sky.

CASTLE OF INDOLENCE

In the bosom of one of those spacious coves which indent the eastern shore of the Hudson, at that broad expansion of the river denominated by the ancient Dutch navigators the Tappan Zee, and where they always prudently shortened sail, and implored the protection of St Nicholas when they crossed, there lies a small market town or rural port, which by some is called Greensburgh, but which is more generally and properly known by the name of Tarry Town. This name was given, we are told, in former days, by the good house-wives of the adjacent country, from the inveterate propensity of their husbands to linger about the village tavern on market days. Be that as it may, I do not vouch for the fact, but merely advert to it, for the sake of being precise and authentic. Not far from this village, perhaps about two miles, there is a little valley, or rather lap of land, among high hills, which is one of the quietest places in the whole world. A small brook glides through it, with just murmur enough to lull one to repose; and the occasional whistle of a quail or tapping of a woodpecker is almost the only sound that ever breaks in upon the uniform tranquillity.

I recollect that, when a stripling, my first exploit in squirrel shooting was in a grove of tall walnut trees that shades one side of the valley. I had wandered into it at noontime, when all nature is peculiarly quiet, and was startled by the roar of my own gun, as it broke the Sabbath stillness around, and was prolonged and reverberated by the angry echoes. If ever I should wish for a retreat, whither I might steal from the world and its distractions and dream quietly away the remnant of a troubled life, I know of none more promising than this little valley.

From the listless repose of the place, and the peculiar character of its inhabitants, who are descendants from the original Dutch settlers, this sequestered glen has long been known by the name of SLEEPY HOLLOW, and its rustic lads are called the Sleepy Hollow Boys throughout all the neighbouring country. A drowsy, dreamy influence seems to hang over the land, and to pervade the very atmosphere. Some say that the place was bewitched by a high German doctor during the early days of the settlement; others, that an old Indian chief, the prophet or wizard of his tribe, held his powwows there before the country was discovered by Master Hendrick Hudson. Certain it is, the place still continues under the sway of some witching power that holds a spell over the minds of the good people, causing them to walk in a continual reverie. They are given to all kinds of marvellous beliefs, are subject to trances and visions, and frequently see strange sights, and hear music and voices in the air. The whole neighbourhood abounds with local tales, haunted spots, and twilight superstitions; stars shoot and meteors glare oftener across the valley than in any other part of the country, and the nightmare, with her whole ninefold, seems to make it the favourite scene of her gambols.

The dominant spirit, however, that haunts this enchanted region and seems to be commander-in-chief of all the powers of the air is the apparition of a figure on horseback without a head. It is said by some to be the ghost of a Hessian trooper, whose head had been carried away by a cannon ball, in some nameless battle during the Revolutionary War, and who is ever and anon seen by the country folk, hurrying along in the gloom of night, as if on the wings of the wind. His haunts are not confined to the valley, but extend at times to the adjacent roads, and especially to the vicinity of a church at no great distance. Indeed, certain of the most authentic historians of those parts, who have been careful in collecting and collating the floating facts concerning this spectre, allege that the body of the trooper, having been buried in the churchyard, the ghost rides forth to the scene of battle in nightly quest of his head; and that the rushing speed with which he sometimes passes along the Hollow, like a midnight blast, is owing to his being belated, and in a hurry to get back to the churchyard before daybreak.

Such is the general purport of this legendary superstition, which has furnished materials for many a wild story in that region of shadows; and the spectre is known, at all the country firesides, by the name of the Headless Horseman of Sleepy Hollow.

It is remarkable that the visionary propensity I have mentioned is not confined to the native inhabitants of the valley, but is unconsciously imbibed by everyone who resides there for a time. However wide awake they may have been before they entered that sleepy region, they are sure, in a little time, to inhale the witching influence of the air, and begin to grow imaginative – to dream dreams and see apparitions.

I mention this peaceful spot with all possible laud; for it is in such little retired Dutch valleys, found here and there embosomed in the great State of New York, that population, manners, and customs remain fixed; while the great torrent of migration and improvement, which is making such incessant changes in other parts of this restless country, sweeps by them unobserved. They are like those little nooks of still water which border a rapid stream, where we may see the straw and bubble riding quietly at anchor, or slowly revolving in their mimic harbour, undisturbed by the rush of the passing current. Though many years have elapsed since I trod the drowsy shades of Sleepy Hollow, yet I question whether I should not still find the same trees and the same families vegetating in its sheltered bosom.

In this by-place of nature there abode, in a remote period of American history, that is to say, some thirty years since, a worthy wight of the name of Ichabod Crane, who sojourned, or, as he expressed it, 'tarried', in Sleepy Hollow, for the purpose of instructing the children of the vicinity. He was a native of Connecticut, a State which supplies the Union with pioneers for the mind as well as for the forest, and sends forth yearly its legions of frontier woodsmen and country schoolmasters. The cognomen of Crane was not inapplicable to his person. He was tall, but exceedingly lank, with narrow shoulders, long arms and legs, hands that dangled a mile out of his sleeves, feet that might have served for shovels, and his whole frame most loosely hung together. His head was small, and flat at top, with huge ears, large green glassy eyes, and a long snipe nose, so that it looked like a weathercock, perched upon his spindle neck, to tell which way the wind blew. To see him striding along the profile of a hill on a windy day, with his clothes bagging and fluttering about him, one might have mistaken him for the genius of famine descending upon the earth, or some scarecrow eloped from a cornfield.

His schoolhouse was a low building of one large room, rudely constructed of logs, the windows partly glazed, and partly patched with leaves of old copybooks. It was most ingeniously secured at vacant hours by a withe twisted in the handle of the door and stakes set against the window shutters, so that, though a thief might get in with perfect ease, he would find some embarrassment in getting out; an idea most probably borrowed by the architect, Yost Van Houten, from the mystery of an eel pot. The schoolhouse stood in a rather lonely but pleasant situation, just at the foot of a woody hill, with a brook running close by, and a formidable birch tree growing at one end of it. From hence the low murmur of his pupils' voices, conning over their lessons, might be heard in a drowsy summer's day, like the hum of a beehive, interrupted now and then by the authoritative voice of the master, in the tone of menace or command, or, peradventure, by the appalling sound of the birch, as he urged some tardy loiterer along the flowery path of knowledge. Truth to say, he was a conscientious man, and ever bore in mind the golden maxim, 'Spare the rod and spoil the child.' Ichabod Crane's scholars certainly were not spoiled.

I would not have it imagined, however, that he was one of those cruel potentates of the school

who joy in the smart of their subjects; on the
contrary, he administered justice with discrimina-
tion rather than severity, taking the burthen off
the backs of the weak, and laying it on those of
the strong. Your mere puny stripling that winced
at the least flourish of the rod was passed by with
indulgence; but the claims of justice were satisfied
by inflicting a double portion on some little,
tough, wrong-headed, broad-skirted Dutch urchin,
who sulked and swelled and grew dogged and
sullen beneath the birch. All this he called 'doing
his duty by their parents'; and he never inflicted a
chastisement without following it by the assurance, so consolatory to the smarting urchin, that
'he would remember it, and thank him for it the
longest day he had to live'.

When school hours were over, he was even the
companion and playmate of the larger boys; and
on holiday afternoons would convoy some of the
smaller ones home, who happened to have pretty
sisters, or good housewives for mothers, noted for
the comforts of the cupboard. Indeed it behooved
him to keep on good terms with his pupils. The
revenue arising from his school was small, and
would have been scarcely sufficient to furnish him
with daily bread, for he was a huge feeder, and
though lank, had the dilating powers of an ana-
conda; but to help out his maintenance, he was,
according to country custom in those parts,
boarded and lodged at the houses of the farmers
whose children he instructed. With these he lived

successively a week at a time; thus going the rounds of the neighbourhood, with all his worldly effects tied up in a cotton handkerchief.

That all this might not be too onerous on the purses of his rustic patrons, who are apt to consider the costs of schooling a grievous burden and school-masters as mere drones, he had various ways of rendering himself both useful and agreeable. He assisted the farmers occasionally in the lighter labours of their farms, helped to make hay, mended the fences, took the horses to water, drove the cows from pasture, and cut wood for the winter fire. He laid aside, too, all the dominant dignity and absolute sway with which he lorded it in his little empire, the school, and became wonderfully gentle and ingratiating. He found favour in the eyes of the mothers by petting the children, particularly the youngest, and would sit with a child on one knee, and rock a cradle with his foot for whole hours together.

In addition to his other vocations, he was the singing master of the neighbourhood, and picked up many bright shillings by instructing the young folks in psalmody. It was a matter of no little vanity to him, on Sundays, to take his station in front of the church gallery, with a band of chosen singers; where, in his own mind, he completely carried away the palm from the parson. Certain it is, his voice resounded far above all the rest of the congregation; and there are peculiar quavers still to be heard in that church, and which may even be heard half a mile off, quite to the opposite side of the millpond, on a still Sunday morning, which are said to be legitimately descended from the nose of Ichabod Crane. Thus, by diverse little makeshifts in that ingenious way which is commonly denominated 'by hook and by crook', the worthy pedagogue got on tolerably enough, and was thought, by all who understood nothing of the labour of headwork, to have a wonderfully easy life of it.

The schoolmaster is generally a man of some importance in the female circle of a rural neighbourhood, being considered a kind of idle gentlemanlike personage, of vastly superior taste and accomplishments to the rough country swains, and, indeed, inferior in learning only to the parson. His appearance, therefore, is apt to occasion some little stir at the tea table of a farmhouse, and the addition of a supernumerary dish of cakes or sweetmeats, or, peradventure, the parade of a silver teapot. Our man of letters, therefore, was peculiarly happy in the smiles of all the country damsels. How he would figure among them in the churchyard, between services on Sundays gathering grapes for them from the wild vines that overrun the surrounding trees, reciting for their amusement all the epitaphs on the tombstones, or sauntering, with a whole bevy of them, along the banks of the adjacent millpond, while the more bashful country bumpkins hung sheepishly back, envying his superior elegance and address.

From his half-itinerant life, also, he was a kind of travelling gazette, carrying the whole budget of local gossip from house to house, so that his appearance was always greeted with satisfaction. He was, moreover, esteemed by the women as a man of great erudition, for he had read several books quite through, and was a perfect master of Cotton Mather's *History of New England Witch-craft,* in which, by the way, he most firmly and potently believed.

He was, in fact, an odd mixture of small shrewdness and simple credulity. His appetite for the marvellous, and his powers of digesting it, were equally extraordinary; and both had been increased by his residence in this spellbound region. No tale was too gross or monstrous for his capacious swallow. It was often his delight, after his school was dismissed in the afternoon, to stretch himself on the rich bed of clover, bordering the little brook that whimpered by his schoolhouse, and there con over old Mather's direful tales, until the gathering dusk of the evening made the printed page a mere mist before his eyes. Then, as he wended his way, by swamp and stream and awful woodland, to the farmhouse where he happened to be quartered, every sound of nature, at that witching hour, fluttered his excited imagination: the moan of the whippoorwill* from the hillside; the boding cry of the tree toad, that

---

* The whippoorwill is a bird which is only heard at night. It receives its name from its note, which is thought to resemble those words.

harbinger of storm; the dreary hooting of the screech owl, or the sudden rustling in the thicket of birds frightened from their roost. The fireflies, too, which sparkled most vividly in the darkest places, now and then startled him, as one of uncommon brightness would stream across his path; and if, by chance, a huge blockhead of a beetle came winging his blundering flight against him, the poor varlet was ready to give up the ghost, with the idea that he was struck with a witch's token. His only resource on such occasions, either to drown thought or drive away evil spirits, was to sing psalm tunes; and the good people of Sleepy Hollow, as they sat by their doors of an evening, were often filled with awe, at hearing his nasal melody, 'in linked sweetness long drawn out', floating from the distant hill or along the dusky road.

Another of his sources of fearful pleasure was to pass long winter evenings with the old Dutch wives as they sat spinning by the fire, with a row of apples roasting and spluttering along the hearth, and listen to their marvellous tales of ghosts and goblins, and haunted fields, and haunted brooks, and haunted bridges, and haunted houses, and particularly of the headless horseman, or galloping Hessian of the Hollow, as they sometimes called him. He would delight them equally by his anecdotes of witchcraft, and of the direful omens and portentous sights and sounds in the air, which prevailed in the earlier times of Connecticut; and would frighten them woefully with speculations upon comets and shooting stars, and with the alarming fact that the world did absolutely turn around, and that they were half the time topsy-turvy!

But if there was a pleasure in all this, while snugly cuddling in the chimney corner of a chamber that was all a ruddy glow from the crackling wood fire, and where, of course, no spectre dared to show his face, it was dearly purchased by the terrors of his subsequent walk homewards. What fearful shapes and shadows beset his path amidst the dim and ghastly glare of a snowy night! With what wistful look did he eye every trembling ray of light streaming across the waste fields from some distant window! How often was he appalled by some shrub covered with snow, which, like a sheeted spectre, beset his very path! How often did he shrink with curdling awe at the sound of his own steps on the frosty crust beneath his feet; and dread to look over his shoulder, lest he should behold some uncouth being tramping close behind him! And how often was he thrown into complete dismay by some rushing blast, howling among the trees, in the idea that it was the Galloping Hessian on one of his nightly scourings!

All these, however, were mere terrors of the night, phantoms of the mind that walk in darkness; and though he had seen many spectres in his time, and been more than once beset by Satan in diverse shapes, in his lonely perambulations, yet daylight put an end to all these evils; and he would have passed a pleasant life of it, in despite of the devil and all his works, if his path had not been crossed by a being that causes more perplexity to mortal man than ghosts, goblins, and the whole race of witches put together, and that was – a woman.

Among the musical disciples who assembled, one evening in each week, to receive his instructions in psalmody, was Katrina Van Tassel, the daughter and only child of a substantial Dutch farmer. She was a blooming lass of fresh eighteen, plump as a partridge, ripe and melting and rosy-cheeked as one of her father's peaches, and universally famed, not merely for her beauty, but her vast expectations. She was withal a little of a coquette, as might be perceived even in her dress, which was a mixture of ancient and modern fashions, as most suited to set off her charms. She wore the ornaments of pure yellow gold, which her great-great-grandmother had brought over from Saardam; the tempting stomacher of the olden time; and withal a provokingly short petticoat, to display the prettiest foot and ankle in the country around.

Ichabod Crane had a soft and foolish heart toward the sex; and it is not to be wondered at that so tempting a morsel soon found favour in his eyes, more especially after he had visited her in her paternal mansion. Old Baltus Van Tassel was a perfect picture of a thriving, contented, liberal-hearted farmer. He seldom, it is true, sent either his eyes or his thoughts beyond the boundaries of his own farm; but within those everything was snug, happy, and well-conditioned. He was satisfied with his wealth, but not proud of it; and piqued himself upon the hearty abundance, rather than the style in which he lived. His stronghold was situated on the banks of the Hudson, in one of those green, sheltered, fertile nooks, in which the Dutch farmers are so fond of nestling. A great elm tree spread its broad branches over it, at the foot of which bubbled up a spring of the softest and sweetest water, in a little well, formed of a barrel, and then stole sparkling away through the grass, to a neighbouring brook that bubbled along among alders and dwarf willows. Hard by the farmhouse was a vast barn that might have served for a church; every window and crevice of which seemed bursting forth with the treasures of the farm; the flail was busily resounding within it from morning to night; swallows and martins skimmed twittering about the eaves; and rows of pigeons, some with one eye turned up, as if watching the weather, some with their heads under their wings, or buried in their bosoms, and others swelling, and cooing, and bowing about their dames, were enjoying the sunshine on the roof. Sleek unwieldy porkers were grunting in the repose and abundance of their pens; whence sallied forth, now and then, troops of sucking pigs, as if to snuff the air. A stately squadron of snowy geese were riding in an adjoining pond, convoying whole fleets of ducks; regiments of turkeys were gobbling through the farmyard, and guinea fowls fretting about it with their peevish discontented cry. Before the barn door strutted the gallant cock, that pattern of a husband, a warrior, and a fine gentleman, clapping his burnished wings and crowing in the pride and gladness of his heart – sometimes tearing up the earth with his feet, and then generously calling his ever-hungry family of wives and children to enjoy the rich morsel which he had discovered.

The pedagogue's mouth watered as he looked upon this sumptuous promise of luxurious winter fare. In his devouring mind's eye he pictured to himself every roasting pig running about with a pudding in his belly and an apple in his mouth; the pigeons were snugly put to bed in a comfortable pie, and tucked in with a coverlet of crust; the geese were swimming in their own gravy; and the ducks pairing cosily in dishes, like snug married couples, with a decent competency of onion sauce. In the porkers he saw carved out the future sleek side of bacon, and juicy relishing ham; not a turkey but he beheld daintily trussed up, with its gizzard under its wing, and, peradventure, a necklace of savoury sausages; and even bright chanticleer himself lay sprawling on his back, in a side-dish, with uplifted claws, as if craving that quarter which his chivalrous spirit disdained to ask while living.

As the enraptured Ichabod fancied all this, and as he rolled his great green eyes over the fat meadow lands, the rich fields of wheat, of rye, of buckwheat, and Indian corn, and the orchards burthened with ruddy fruit, which surrounded the warm tenement of Van Tassel, his heart yearned after the damsel who was to inherit these domains, and his imagination expanded with the idea how they might be readily turned into cash, and the money invested in immense tracts of wild land, and shingle palaces in the wilderness. Nay, his busy fancy already realized his hopes, and presented to him the blooming Katrina, with a whole family of children, mounted on the top of a wagon loaded with household trumpery, with pots and kettles dangling beneath; and he beheld himself bestriding a pacing mare, with a colt at her heels, setting out for Kentucky, Tennessee, or the Lord knows where.

When he entered the house the conquest of his heart was complete. It was one of those spacious farmhouses, with high-ridged, but lowly sloping roofs, built in the style handed down from the first Dutch settlers, the low projecting eaves forming a piazza along the front, capable of being closed up in bad weather. Under this were hung flails, harness, various utensils of husbandry, and nets for fishing in the neighbouring river. Benches were built along the sides for summer use; and a great spinning wheel at one end, and a churn at the other, showed the various uses to which this important porch might be devoted. From this piazza the wondering Ichabod entered the hall, which formed the centre of the mansion and the place of usual residence. Here, rows of resplendent pewter, ranged on a long dresser, dazzled his eyes. In one corner stood a huge bag of wool ready to be spun; in another a quantity of linsey-woolsey just from the loom; ears of Indian corn and strings of dried apples and peaches hung in gay festoons along the walls, mingled with the gaud of red peppers; and a door left ajar gave him a peep into the best parlour, where the claw-footed chairs and dark mahogany tables shone like mirrors; and irons, with their accompanying shovel and tongs, glistened from their covert of asparagus tops; mock oranges and conch shells decorated the mantelpiece; strings of various coloured birds' eggs were suspended above it; a great ostrich egg was hung from the centre of the room, and a corner cupboard, knowingly left open, displayed immense treasures of old silver and well-mended china.

From the moment Ichabod laid his eyes upon these regions of delight, the peace of his mind was at an end, and his only study was how to gain the affections of the peerless daughter of Van Tassel. In this enterprise, however, he had more real difficulties than generally fell to the lot of a knight-errant of yore, who seldom had anything but giants, enchanters, fiery dragons, and such like easily conquered adversaries to contend with;

and had to make his way merely through gates of iron and brass, and walls of adamant, to the castle keep, where the lady of his heart was confined; all which he achieved as easily as a man would carve his way to the centre of a Christmas pie; and then the lady gave him her hand as a matter of course. Ichabod, on the contrary, had to win his way to the heart of a country coquette, beset with a labyrinth of whims and caprices, which were forever presenting new difficulties and impediments; and he had to encounter a host of fearful adversaries of real flesh and blood, the numerous rustic admirers, who beset every portal to her heart, keeping a watchful and angry eye upon each other, but ready to fly out in the common cause against any new competitor.

Among these the most formidable was a burly, roaring, roystering blade, of the name of Abraham, or, according to the Dutch abbreviation, Brom Van Brunt, the hero of the country round, which rang with his feats of strength and hardihood. He was broad-shouldered and double-jointed, with short curly black hair, and a bluff but not unpleasant countenance, having a mingled air of fun and arrogance. From his Herculean frame and great powers of limb, he had received the nickname of BROM BONES, by which he was universally known. He was famed for great knowledge and skill in horsemanship, being as dexterous on horseback as a Tartar. He was foremost at all races and cockfights; and, with the ascendency which bodily

strength acquires in rustic life, was the umpire in
all disputes, setting his hat on one side and giving
his decisions with an air and tone admitting of no
gainsay or appeal. He was always ready for either
a fight or a frolic; but had more mischief than ill
will in his composition, and, with all his overbear-
ing roughness, there was a strong dash of waggish
good humour at bottom. He had three or four
boon companions, who regarded him as their
model and at the head of whom he scoured the
country, attending every scene of feud or merri-
ment for miles around. In cold weather he was
distinguished by a fur cap, surmounted with a
flaunting fox's tail; and when the folks at a country
gathering described this well-known crest at a
distance, whisking about among a squad of hard
riders, they always stood by for a squall. Sometimes his crew would be heard dashing along past
the farmhouses at midnight, with whoop and
halloo, like a troop of Don Cossacks; and the old
dames, startled out of their sleep, would listen for
a moment till the hurry-scurry had clattered by,
and then exclaim, 'Ay, there goes Brom Bones
and his gang!' The neighbours looked, upon him
with a mixture of awe, admiration, and good will;
and when any madcap prank or rustic brawl occurred in the vicinity, always shook their heads
and warranted Brom Bones was at the bottom
of it.

This rantipole hero had for some time singled
out the blooming Katrina for the object of his

uncouth gallantries, and though his amorous toy-
ings were something like the gentle caresses and
endearments of a bear, yet it was whispered that
she did not altogether discourage his hopes. Certain it is, his advances were signals for rival candi-
date's to retire, who felt no inclination to cross a
lion in his amours; insomuch, that when his horse
was seen tied to Van Tassel's paling, on a Sunday
night, a sure sign that his master was courting, or,
as it is termed, 'sparking', within, all other suitors
passed by in despair, and carried the war into
other quarters.

Such was the formidable rival with whom Ichabod Crane had to contend, and, considering all
things, a stouter man than he would have shrunk
from the competition, and a wiser man would
have despaired. He had, however, a happy mixture
of pliability and perseverance in his nature; he
was in form and spirit like a supple jack – yielding,
but tough; though he bent, he never broke; and
though he bowed beneath the slightest pressure,
yet, the moment it was away – jerk! he was as
erect, and carried his head as high as ever.

To have taken the field openly against his rival
would have been madness, for he was not a man
to be thwarted in his amours. Ichabod, therefore,
made his advances in a quiet and gently insinuat-
ing manner. Under cover of his character of singing master, he made frequent visits to the farmhouse; not that he had anything to apprehend from
the meddlesome interference of parents, which is

so often a stumbling block in the path of lovers.
Balt Van Tassel was an easy indulgent soul; he
loved his daughter better even than his pipe, and,
like a reasonable man and an excellent father, let
her have her way in everything. His notable wife,
too, had enough to do to attend to her housekeep-
ing and manage her poultry; for, as she sagely
observed, ducks and geese are foolish things, and
must be looked after, but girls can take care of
themselves. Thus while the busy dame bustled
about the house, or plied her spinning wheel at
one end of the piazza, honest Balt would sit smoking his evening pipe at the other, watching the
achievements of a little wooden warrior, who,
armed with a sword in each hand, was most val-
iantly fighting the wind on the pinnacle of the
barn. In the meantime, Ichabod would carry on
his suit with the daughter by the side of the
spring under the great elm, or sauntering along in
the twilight, that hour so favourable to the lover's
eloquence.

I profess not to know how women's hearts are
wooed and won. To me they have always been
matters of riddle and admiration. Some seem to
have but one vulnerable point, or door of access,
while others have a thousand avenues, and may be
captured in a thousand different ways. It is a great
triumph of skill to gain the former, but a still
greater proof of generalship to maintain possession
of the latter, for the man must battle for his
fortress at every door and window. He who wins a

thousand common hearts is therefore entitled to some renown; but he who keeps undisputed sway over the heart of a coquette is indeed a hero. Certain it is, this was not the case with the redoubtable Brom Bones; and from the moment Ichabod Crane made his advances, the interests of the former evidently declined; his horse was no longer seen tied at the palings on Sunday nights, and a deadly feud gradually arose between him and the preceptor of Sleepy Hollow.

Brom, who had a degree of rough chivalry in his nature, would fain have carried matters to open warfare, and have settled their pretensions to the lady according to the mode of those most concise and simple reasoners, the knights-errant of yore – by single combat; but Ichabod was too conscious of the superior might of his adversary to enter the lists against him. He had overheard a boast of Bones that he would 'double the school-master up, and lay him on a shelf of his own schoolhouse', and he was too wary to give him an opportunity. There was something extremely provoking in this obstinately pacific system; it left Brom no alternative but to draw upon the funds of rustic waggery in his disposition, and to play off boorish practical jokes upon his rival. Ichabod became the object of whimsical persecution to Bones and his gang of rough riders. They harried his hitherto peaceful domains; smoked out his singing school by stopping up the chimney; broke into the schoolhouse at night, in spite of its formidable fastenings of withe and window stakes, and turned everything topsy-turvy, so that the poor schoolmaster began to think all the witches in the country held their meetings there. But what was still more annoying, Brom took all opportunities of turning him into ridicule in presence of his mistress, and had a scoundrel dog whom he taught to whine in the most ludicrous manner, and introduced as a rival of Ichabod's to instruct her in psalmody.

In this way matters went on for some time, without producing any material effect on the relative situation of the contending powers. On a fine autumnal afternoon, Ichabod, in pensive mood, sat enthroned on the lofty stool whence he usually watched all the concerns of his little literary realm. In his hand he swayed a ferule, that sceptre of despotic power; the birch of justice reposed on three nails, behind the throne, a constant terror to evil-doers; while on the desk before him might be seen sundry contraband articles and prohibited weapons, detected upon the persons of idle urchins, such as half-munched apples, popguns, whirligigs, fly cages, and whole legions of rampant little paper gamecocks. Apparently there had been some appalling act of justice recently inflicted, for his scholars were all busily intent upon their books, or slyly whispering behind them with one eye kept upon the master; and a kind of buzzing stillness reigned throughout the schoolroom. It was suddenly interrupted by the appearance of a

Negro, in tow-cloth jacket and trousers, a round-crowned fragment of a hat, like the cap of Mercury, and mounted on the back of a ragged, wild, half-broken colt, which he managed with a rope by way of halter. He came clattering up to the school door with an invitation to Ichabod to attend a merrymaking or 'quilting frolic' to be held that evening at Mynheer Van Tassel's and having delivered his message he dashed over the brook and was seen scampering away up the hollow, full of the importance and hurry of his mission.

All was now bustle and hubbub in the late quiet schoolroom. The scholars were hurried through their lessons, without stopping at trifles; those who were nimble skipped over half with impunity, and those who were tardy had a smart application now and then in the rear to quicken their speed or help them over a tall word. Books were flung aside without being put away on the shelves, inkstands were overturned, benches thrown down, and the whole school was turned loose an hour before the usual time, bursting forth like a legion of young imps, yelping and racketing about the green, in joy at their early emancipation.

The gallant Ichabod now spent at least an extra half hour at his toilet, brushing and furbishing up his best and indeed only suit of rusty black, and arranging his looks by a bit of broken looking glass that hung up in the schoolhouse. That he might make his appearance before his mistress in the true style of a cavalier he borrowed a horse from the farmer with whom he was domiciliated, a choleric old Dutchman of the name of Hans Van Ripper, and, thus gallantly mounted, issued forth, like a knight-errant in quest of adventures. But it is meet I should, in the true spirit of romantic story, give some account of the looks and equipments of my hero and his steed. The animal he bestrode was a broken-down plough horse that had outlived almost everything but his viciousness. He was gaunt and shagged, with a ewe neck and a head like a hammer; his rusty mane and tail were tangled and knotted with burrs; one eye had lost its pupil and was glaring and spectral, but the other had the gleam of a genuine devil in it. Still he must have had fire and mettle in his day, if we may judge from the name he bore of Gunpowder. He had, in fact, been a favourite steed of his master's, the choleric Van Ripper, who was a furious rider, and had infused, very probably, some of his own spirit into the animal, for, old and broken-down as he looked, there was more of the lurking evil in him than in any young filly in the country.

Ichabod was a suitable figure for such a steed. He rode with short stirrups, which brought his knees nearly up to the pommel of the saddle; his sharp elbows stuck out like grasshoppers'; he carried his whip perpendicularly in his hand, like a sceptre, and, as his horse jogged on, the motion of his arms was not unlike the flapping of a pair of wings. A small wool hat rested on the top of his nose, for so his scanty strip of forehead might be called; and the skirts of his black coat fluttered out almost to the horse's tail. Such was the appearance of Ichabod and his steed, as they shambled out of the gate of Hans Van Ripper, and it was altogether such an apparition as is seldom to be met with in broad daylight.

It was, as I have said, a fine autumnal day, the sky was clear and serene, and nature wore that rich and golden livery which we always associate with the idea of abundance. The forests had put on their sober brown and yellow, while some trees of the tenderer kind had been nipped by the frosts into brilliant dyes of orange, purple, and scarlet. Streaming files of wild ducks began to make their appearance high in the air; the bark of the squirrel might be heard from the groves of beech and hickory nuts, and the pensive whistle of the quail at intervals from the neighbouring stubble field.

The small birds were taking their farewell banquets. In the fullness of their revelry, they fluttered, chirping and frolicking, from bush to bush, and tree to tree, capricious from the very profusion and variety around them. There was the honest cock robin, the favourite game of stripling sportsmen, with its loud querulous note; and the twittering blackbirds flying in sable clouds; and the golden-winged woodpecker, with his crimson

crest, his broad black gorget, and splendid plum-
age; and the cedar bird, with its red-tipped wings
and yellow-tipped tail, and its little monteiro cap
of feathers; and the blue jay, that noisy coxcomb,
in his gay light-blue coat and white under-clothes;
screaming and chattering, nodding and bobbing
and bowing, and pretending to be on good terms
with every songster of the grove.

As Ichabod jogged slowly on his way, his eye,
ever open to every symptom of culinary abundance, ranged with delight over the treasures of
jolly autumn. On all sides he beheld vast store of
apples, some hanging in oppressive opulence on
the trees, some gathered into baskets and barrels
for the market, others heaped up in rich piles for
the cider press. Farther on he beheld great fields
of Indian corn, with its golden ears peeping from
their leafy coverts and holding out the promise of
cakes and hasty pudding; and the yellow pumpkins
lying beneath them, turning up their fair round
bellies to the sun, and giving ample prospects of
the most luxurious of pies; and anon he passed the
fragrant buckwheat fields, breathing the odour of
the beehive, and as he beheld them, soft anticipations stole over his mind of dainty slapjacks, well
buttered and garnished with honey or treacle, by
the delicate little dimpled hand of Katrina Van
Tassel.

Thus feeding his mind with many sweet
thoughts and 'sugared suppositions', he journeyed
along the sides of a range of hills which look out

upon some of the goodliest scenes of the mighty Hudson. The sun gradually wheeled his broad disc down into the west. The wide bosom of the Tappan Zee lay motionless and glassy, excepting that here and there a gentle undulation waved and prolonged the blue shadow of the distant mountain. A few amber clouds floated in the sky, without a breath of air to move them. The horizon was of a fine golden tint, changing gradually into a pure apple green, and from that into the deep blue of the mid-heaven. A slanting ray lingered on the woody crests of the precipices that overhung some parts of the river, giving greater depth to the dark-grey and purple of their rocky sides. A sloop was loitering in the distance, dropping slowly down with the tide, her sail hanging uselessly against the mast; and as the reflection of the sky gleamed along the still water, it seemed as if the vessel was suspended in the air.

It was toward evening that Ichabod arrived at the castle of the Heer Van Tassel, which he found thronged with the pride and flower of the adjacent country. Old farmers, a spare leathern-faced race, in homespun coats and breeches, blue stockings, huge shoes, and magnificent pewter buckles. Their brisk withered little dames, in close-crimped caps, long-waisted short gowns, homespun petticoats, with scissors and pincushions and gay calico pockets hanging on the outside. Buxom lasses, almost as antiquated as their mothers, excepting where a straw hat, a fine ribbon, or perhaps a white frock gave symptoms of city innovation. The sons, in short square-skirted coats with rows of stupendous brass buttons, and their hair generally queued in the fashion of the times, especially if they could procure an eel skin for the purpose, it being esteemed throughout the country as a potent nourisher and strengthener of the hair.

Brom Bones, however, was the hero of the scene, having come to the gathering on his favourite steed Daredevil, creature, like himself, full of mettle and mischief, and which no one but himself could manage. He was, in fact, noted for preferring vicious animals, given to all kinds of tricks, which kept the rider in constant risk of his neck, for he held a tractable well-broken horse as unworthy of a lad of spirit.

Fain would I pause to dwell upon the world of charms that burst upon the enraptured gaze of my hero as he entered the state parlour of Van Tassel's mansion. Not those of the bevy of buxom lasses, with their luxurious display of red and white, but the ample charms of a genuine Dutch country tea table, in the sumptuous time of autumn. Such heaped-up platters of cakes of various and almost indescribable kinds, known only to experienced Dutch housewives! There was the doughty dough-nut, the tenderer oly koek, and the crisp and crumbling cruller; sweet cakes and shortcakes, ginger cakes and honey cakes, and the whole family of cakes. And then there were apple pies and peach pies and pumpkin pies; besides slices of ham and smoked beef and moreover delectable dishes of preserved plums, and peaches, and pears, and quinces; not to mention broiled shad and roasted chickens; together with bowls of milk and cream, all mingled higgledy-piggledy, pretty much as I have enumerated them, with the motherly teapot sending up its clouds of vapour from the midst – Heaven bless the mark! I want breath and time to discuss this banquet as it deserves, and am too eager to get on with my story. Happily, Ichabod Crane was not in so great a hurry as his historian, but did ample justice to every dainty.

He was a kind and thankful creature whose heart dilated in proportion as his skin was filled with good cheer, and whose spirits rose with eating as some men's do with drink. He could not help, too, rolling his large eyes around him as he ate, and chuckling with the possibility that he might one day be lord of all this scene of almost unimaginable luxury and splendour. Then, he thought, how soon he'd turn his back upon the old schoolhouse; snap his fingers in the face of Hans Van Ripper, and every other niggardly patron, and kick any itinerant pedagogue out of doors that should dare to call him comrade!

Old Baltus Van Tassel moved about among his guests with a face dilated with content and good humour, round and jolly as the harvest moon. His hospitable attentions were brief, but expressive, being confined to a shake of the hand, a slap on the shoulder, a loud laugh, and a pressing invitation to 'fall to, and help themselves'.

And now the sound of the music from the common room, or hall, summoned to the dance. The musician was an old grey-headed Negro, who had been the itinerant orchestra of the neighbourhood for more than half a century. His instrument was as old and battered as himself. The greater part of the time he scraped on two or three strings, accompanying every movement of the bow with a motion of the head; bowing almost to the ground and stamping with his foot whenever a fresh couple were to start.

Ichabod prided himself upon his dancing as much as upon his vocal powers. Not a limb, not a fibre about him was idle; and to have seen his loosely hung frame in full motion, and clattering about the room, you would have thought Saint Vitus himself, that blessed patron of the dance, was figuring before you in person. He was the admiration of all the Negroes, who, having gathered, of all ages and sizes, from the farm and the neighbourhood, stood forming a pyramid of faces at every door and window, gazing with delight at the scene. How could the flogger of urchins be otherwise than animated and joyous? The lady of his heart was his partner in the dance, and smiling graciously in reply to all his amorous oglings, while Brom Bones, sorely smitten with love and jealousy, sat brooding by himself in one corner.

When the dance was at an end, Ichabod was

attracted to a knot of the sager folks, who, with old Van Tassel, sat smoking at one end of the piazza, gossiping over former times, and drawing out long stories about the war.

This neighbourhood, at the time of which I am speaking, was one of those highly favoured places which abound with chronicle and great men. The British and American line had run near it during the war; it had, therefore, been the scene of marauding, and infested with refugees, cowboys, and all kinds of border chivalry. Just sufficient time had elapsed to enable each storyteller to dress up his tale with a little becoming fiction, and, in the indistinctness of his recollection, to make himself the hero of every exploit.

There was the story of Doffue Martling, a large blue-bearded Dutchman, who had nearly taken a British frigate with an old iron nine-pounder from a mud breastwork, only that his gun burst at the sixth discharge. And there was an old gentleman who shall be nameless, being too rich a mynheer to be lightly mentioned, who, in the Battle of White Plains, being an excellent master of defence, parried a musket ball with a small sword, insomuch that he absolutely felt it whizz around the blade and glance off at the hilt, in proof of which he was ready at any time to show the sword, with the hilt a little bent. There were several more that had been equally great in the field, not one of whom but was persuaded that he had a considerable hand in bringing the war to a happy termination.

But all these were nothing to the tales of ghosts and apparitions that succeeded. The neighbourhood is rich in legendary treasures of the kind. Local tales and superstitions thrive best in these sheltered long-settled retreats, but are trampled under foot by the shifting throng that forms the population of most of our country places. Besides, there is no encouragement for ghosts in most of our villages, for they have scarcely had time to finish their first nap and turn themselves in their graves before their surviving friends have travelled away from the neighbourhood; so that when they turn out at night to walk their rounds they have no acquaintance left to call upon. This is perhaps the reason why we so seldom hear of ghosts except in our long-established Dutch communities.

The immediate cause, however, of the prevalence of supernatural stories in these parts was doubtless, owing to the vicinity of Sleepy Hollow. There was a contagion in the very air that blew from that haunted region; it breathed forth an atmosphere of dreams and fancies infecting all the land. Several of the Sleepy Hollow people were present at Van Tassel's, and, as usual, were doling out their wild and wonderful legends. Many dismal tales were told about funeral trains, and mourning cries and wailings heard and seen about the great tree where the unfortunate Major André

was taken, and which stood in the neighbourhood. Some mention was made also of the woman
in white that haunted the dark glen at Raven
Rock, and was often heard to shriek on winter
nights before a storm, having perished there in
the snow. The chief part of the stories, however,
turned upon the favourite spectre of Sleepy
Hollow, the headless horseman, who had been
heard several times of late, patrolling the country,
and, it was said, tethered his horse nightly among
the graves in the churchyard.

The sequestered situation of this church seems
always to have made it a favourite haunt of troubled spirits. It stands on a knoll, surrounded by
locust trees and lofty elms, from among which its
decent whitewashed walls shine modestly forth,
like Christian purity beaming through the shades
of retirement. A gentle slope descends from it to a
silver sheet of water, bordered by high trees, between which peeps may be caught at the blue hills
of the Hudson. To look upon its grass-grown
yard, where the sunbeams seem to sleep so quietly,
one would think that there at least the dead might
rest in peace. On one side of the church extends a
wide woody dell, along which raves a large brook
among broken rocks and trunks of fallen trees.
Over a deep black part of the stream, not far from
the church, was formerly thrown a wooden bridge;
the road that led to it, and the bridge itself, were
thickly shaded by overhanging trees, which cast a
gloom about it, even in the daytime, but occa-

sioned a fearful darkness at night. This was one of the favourite haunts of the headless horseman, and the place where he was most frequently encountered. The tale was told of old Brouwer, a most heretical disbeliever in ghosts, how he met the horseman returning from his foray into Sleepy Hollow, and was obliged to get up behind him; how they galloped over bush and brake, over hill and swamp, until they reached the bridge, when the horseman suddenly turned into a skeleton, threw old Brouwer into the brook, and sprang away over the tree tops with a clap of thunder.

This story was immediately matched by a thrice marvellous adventure of Brom Bones, who made light of the galloping Hessian as an arrant jockey. He affirmed that, on returning one night from the neighbouring village of Sing Sing, he had been overtaken by this midnight trooper; that he had offered to race with him for a bowl of punch, and should have won it too, for Daredevil beat the goblin horse all hollow, but, just as they came to the church bridge, the Hessian bolted and vanished in a flash of fire.

All these tales, told in that drowsy undertone with which men talk in the dark, the countenances of the listeners only now and then receiving a casual gleam from the glare of a pipe, sank deep in the mind of Ichabod. He repaid them in kind with large extracts from his invaluable author, Cotton Mather, and added many marvellous events that had taken place in his native State of Connecticut, and fearful sights which he had seen in his nightly walks about Sleepy Hollow.

The revel now gradually broke up. The old farmers gathered together their families in their wagons, and were heard for some time rattling along the hollow roads and over the distant hills. Some of the damsels mounted on pillions behind their favourite swains, and their lighthearted laughter, mingling with the clatter of hoofs, echoed along the silent woodlands, sounding fainter and fainter until they gradually died away – and the late scene of noise and frolic was all silent and deserted. Ichabod only lingered behind, according to the custom of country lovers, to have a tête-à-tête with the heiress, fully convinced that he was now on the high road to success. What passed at this interview I will not pretend to say, for in fact I do not know. Something, however, I fear me, must have gone wrong, for he certainly sallied forth, after no very great interval, with an air quite desolate and chopfallen. Oh these women! these women! Could that girl have been playing off any of her coquettish tricks? Was her encouragement of the poor pedagogue all a mere sham to secure her conquest of his rival? Heaven only knows, not I! Let it suffice to say, Ichabod stole forth with the air of one who had been sacking a hen roost rather than a fair lady's heart. Without looking to the right or left to notice the scene of rural wealth, on which he had so often gloated, he went straight to the stable, and with several hearty

cuffs and kicks roused his steed most uncourt-
eously from the comfortable quarters in which he
was soundly sleeping, dreaming of mountains of
corn and oats, and whole valleys of timothy and
clover.

It was the very witching time of night that
Ichabod, heavyhearted and crestfallen, pursued
his travel homeward, along the sides of the lofty
hills which rise above Tarry Town, and which he
had traversed so cheerily in the afternoon. The
hour was as dismal as himself. Far below him, the
Tappan Zee spread its dusky and indistinct waste
of waters, with here and there the tall mast of a
sloop, riding quietly at anchor under the land. In
the dead hush of midnight he could even hear
the barking of the watchdog from the opposite
shore of the Hudson, but it was so vague and faint
as only to give an idea of his distance from this
faithful companion of man. Now and then, too,
the long-drawn crowing of a cock, accidentally
awakened, would sound far, far off, from some
farmhouse away among the hills – but it was like a
dreaming sound in his ear. No signs of life occurred near him, but occasionally the melancholy
chirp of a cricket, or perhaps the guttural twang
of a bullfrog, from a neighbouring marsh, as if
sleeping uncomfortably and turning suddenly in
his bed.

All the stories of ghosts and goblins that he had
heard in the afternoon now came crowding upon
his recollection. The night grew darker and

darker; the stars seemed to sink deeper in the sky, and driving clouds occasionally hid them from his sight. He had never felt so lonely and dismal. He was, moreover, approaching the very place where many of the scenes of the ghost stories had been laid. In the centre of the road stood an enormous tulip tree, which towered like a giant above all the other trees of the neighbourhood and formed a kind of landmark. Its limbs were gnarled and fantastic, large enough to form trunks for ordinary trees, twisting down almost to the earth and nosing again into the air. It was connected with the tragical story of the unfortunate André, who had been taken prisoner hard by; and was universally known by the name of Major André's tree. The common people regarded it with a mixture of respect and superstition, partly out of sympathy for the fate of its ill-starred namesake, and partly from the tales of strange sights and doleful lamentations told concerning it.

As Ichabod approached this fearful tree, he began to whistle; he thought his whistle was answered – it was but a blast sweeping sharply through the dry branches. As he approached a little nearer, he thought he saw something white hanging in the midst of the tree – he paused and ceased whistling; but on looking more narrowly, perceived that it was a place where the tree had been scathed by lightning and the white wood laid bare. Suddenly he heard a groan – his teeth chattered and his knees smote against the saddle; it

was but the rubbing of one huge bough upon
another as they were swayed about by the breeze.
He passed the tree in safety, but new perils lay
before him.

About two hundred yards from the tree a small
brook crossed the road and ran into a marshy and
thickly wooded glen, known by the name of
Wiley's swamp. A few rough logs, laid side by
side, served for a bridge over this stream. On that
side of the road where the brook entered the
wood, a group of oaks and chestnuts, matted thick
with wild grapevines, threw a cavernous gloom
over it. To pass this bridge was the severest trial.
It was at this identical spot that the unfortunate
André was captured, and under the covert of
those chestnuts and vines were the sturdy yeomen
concealed who surprised him. This has ever since
been considered a haunted stream, and fearful are
the feelings of the schoolboy who has to pass it
alone after dark.

As he approached the stream his heart began to
thump; he summoned up, however, all his resolution, gave his horse half a score of kicks in the
ribs, and attempted to dash briskly across the
bridge; but instead of starting forward, the per-
verse old animal made a lateral movement and ran
broadside against the fence. Ichabod, whose fears
increased with the delay, jerked the reins on the
other side, and kicked lustily with the contrary
foot; it was all in vain; his steed started, it is true,
but it was only to plunge to the opposite side of

the road into a thicket of brambles and alder bushes. The schoolmaster now bestowed both whip and heel upon the starveling ribs of old Gunpowder, who dashed forward, snuffling and snorting, but came to a stand just by the bridge with a suddenness that had nearly sent his rider sprawling over his head. Just at this moment a plashy tramp by the side of the bridge caught the sensitive ear of Ichabod. In the dark shadow of the grove, on the margin of the brook, he beheld something huge, misshapen, black and towering. It stirred not, but seemed gathered up in the gloom, like some gigantic monster ready to spring upon the traveller.

The hair of the affrighted pedagogue rose upon his head with terror. What was to be done? To turn and fly was now too late; and besides, what chance was there of escaping ghost or goblin, if such it was, which could ride upon the wings of the wind? Summoning up, therefore, a show of courage, he demanded in stammering accents – 'Who are you?' He received no reply. He repeated his demand in a still more agitated voice. Still there was no answer. Once more he cudgelled the sides of the inflexible Gunpowder, and, shutting his eyes, broke forth with involuntary fervour into a psalm tune. Just then the shadowy object of alarm put itself in motion, and, with a scramble and a bound, stood at once in the middle of the road. Though the night was dark and dismal, yet the form of the unknown might now in some degree be ascertained. He appeared to be a horse-man of large dimensions, and mounted on a black horse of powerful fame. He made no offer of molestation or sociability, but kept aloof on one side of the road, jogging along on the blind side of old Gunpowder, who had now got over his fright and waywardness.

Ichabod, who had no relish for this strange midnight companion, and bethought himself of the adventure of Brom Bones with the Galloping Hessian, now quickened his steed, in hopes of leaving him behind. The stranger, however, quick-ened his horse to an equal pace. Ichabod pulled up, and fell into a walk, thinking to lag behind – the other did the same. His heart began to sink within him he endeavoured to resume his psalm tune, but his parched tongue clove to the roof of his mouth, and he could not utter a stave. There was something in the moody and dogged silence of this pertinacious companion that was mysteri-ous and appalling. It was soon fearfully accounted for. On mounting a rising ground, which brought the figure of his fellow-traveller in relief against the sky, gigantic in height, and muffled in a cloak, Ichabod was horror-struck on perceiving that he was headless! But his horror was still more in-creased on observing that the head, which should have rested on his shoulders, was carried before him on the pommel of the saddle. His terror rose to desperation; he rained a shower of kicks and blows upon Gunpowder, hoping, by a sudden movement, to give his companion the slip – but the spectre started full jump with him. Away then they dashed, through thick and thin, stones flying and sparks flashing at every bound. Ichabod's flimsy garments fluttered in the air as he stretched his long lank body away over his horse's head, in the eagerness of his flight.

They had now reached the road which turns off to Sleepy Hollow; but Gunpowder, who seemed possessed with a demon, instead of keeping up it, made an opposite turn, and plunged headlong downhill to the left. This road leads through a sandy hollow, shaded by trees for about a quarter of a mile, where it crosses the bridge famous in goblin story, and just beyond swells the green knoll on which stands the whitewashed church.

As yet the panic of the steed had given his unskilful rider an apparent advantage in the chase; but just as he had got halfway through the hollow, the girths of the saddle gave way, and he felt it slipping from under him. He seized it by the pommel and endeavoured to hold it firm, but in vain; and had just time to save himself by clasping old Gunpowder around the neck when the saddle fell to the earth, and he heard it trampled under foot by his pursuer. For a moment the terror of Hans Van Ripper's wrath passed across his mind – for it was his Sunday saddle; but this was no time for petty fears; the goblin was hard on his haunches, and (unskilful rider that he was!) he had much ado to maintain his seat, sometimes slipping on one side, sometimes on the other, and sometimes jolted on the high ridge of his horse's backbone with a violence that he verily feared would cleave him asunder.

An opening in the trees now cheered him with the hopes that the church bridge was at hand. The wavering reflection of a silver star in the bosom of the brook told him that he was not mistaken. He saw the walls of the church dimly glaring under the trees beyond. He recollected the place where Brom Bones's ghostly competitor had disappeared. 'If I can but reach that bridge,' thought Ichabod, 'I am safe.' Just then he heard the black steed panting and blowing close behind him; he even fancied that he felt his hot breath. Another convulsive kick in the ribs and old Gunpowder sprang upon the bridge; he thundered over the resounding planks; he gained the opposite side; and now Ichabod cast a look behind to see if his pursuer should vanish, according to rule, in a flash of fire and brimstone. Just then he saw the goblin rising in his stirrups, and in the very act of hurling his head at him. Ichabod endeavoured to dodge the horrible missile, but too late. It encountered his cranium with a tremendous crash – he was tumbled headlong into the dust, and Gunpowder, the black steed, and the goblin rider, passed by like a whirlwind.

The next morning the old horse was found without his saddle, and with the bridle under his feet, soberly cropping the grass at his master's gate. Ichabod did not make his appearance at breakfast – dinner hour came, but no Ichabod. The boys assembled at the schoolhouse, and strolled idly about the banks of the brook; but no schoolmaster. Hans Van Ripper now began to feel some uneasiness about the fate of poor Ichabod, and his saddle. An inquiry was set on foot, and after diligent investigation they came upon his traces. In one part of the road leading to the church was found the saddle trampled in the dirt; the tracks of horses' hoofs deeply dented in the road, and evidently at furious speed, were traced to the bridge, beyond which, on the bank of a broad part of the brook, where the water ran deep and black, was found the hat of the unfortunate Ichabod, and close beside it a shattered pumpkin.

The brook was searched, but the body of the schoolmaster was not to be discovered. Hans Van Ripper, as executor of his estate, examined the bundle which contained all his worldly effects. They consisted of two shirts and a half, two stocks for the neck, a pair or two of worsted stockings, an old pair of corduroy small clothes, a rusty razor, a book of psalm tunes full of dogs' ears, and a broken pitchpipe. As to the books and furniture of the schoolhouse, they belonged to the community, excepting Cotton Mather's *History of Witchcraft*, *a New England Almanac*, and a book of dreams and fortune-telling; in which last was a sheet of foolscap much scribbled and blotted in several fruitless attempts to make a copy of verses in honour of the heiress of Van Tassel. These magic books and the poetic scrawl were forthwith consigned to the flames by Hans Van Ripper, who from that time forward determined to send his children no more to school, observing that he never knew any good come of this same reading and writing. Whatever money the schoolmaster possessed, and he had received his quarter's pay but a day or two before, he must have had about his person at the time of his disappearance.

The mysterious event caused much speculation at the church on the following Sunday. Knots of gazers and gossips were collected in the church-yard, at the bridge, and at the spot where the hat and pumpkin had been found. The stories of Brouwer, of Bones, and a whole budget of others were called to mind; and when they had diligently considered them all and compared them with the symptoms of the present case, they shook their heads and came to the conclusion that Ichabod had been carried off by the galloping Hessian. As he was a bachelor and in nobody's debt, nobody troubled his head any more about him. The school was removed to a different quarter of the hollow, and another pedagogue reigned in his stead.

It is true an old farmer, who had been down to New York on a visit several years after, and from whom this account of the ghostly adventure was received, brought home the intelligence that Ichabod Crane was still alive; that he had left the neighbourhood, partly through fear of the goblin and Hans Van Ripper, and partly in mortification at having been suddenly dismissed by the heiress; that he had changed his quarters to a distant part of the country, had kept school and studied law at the same time, had been admitted to the bar, turned politician, electioneered, written for the newspapers, and finally had been made a justice of the Ten Pound Court. Brom Bones too, who shortly after his rival's disappearance conducted the blooming Katrina in triumph to the altar, was observed to look exceedingly knowing whenever the story of Ichabod was related, and always burst into a hearty laugh at the mention of the pumpkin, which led some to suspect that he knew more about the matter than he chose to tell.

The old country wives, however, who are the best judges of these matters, maintain to this day that Ichabod was spirited away by supernatural means; and it is a favourite story often told about the neighbourhood around the winter evening fire. The bridge became more than ever an object of superstitious awe, and that may be the reason why the road has been altered of late years, so as to approach the church by the border of the mill-pond. The schoolhouse, being deserted, soon fell to decay, and was reported to be haunted by the ghost of the unfortunate pedagogue; and the ploughboy, loitering homeward of a still summer evening, has often fancied his voice at a distance, chanting a melancholy psalm tune among the tranquil solitudes of Sleepy Hollow.

POSTSCRIPT

FOUND IN THE HANDWRITING OF
MR KNICKERBOCKER

The preceding Tale is given, almost in the precise words in which I heard it related at a Corporation meeting of the ancient city of Manhattoes, at which were present many of its sagest and most illustrious burghers. The narrator was a pleasant, shabby, gentlemanly old fellow, in pepper-and-salt clothes, with a sadly humorous face, and one whom I strongly suspected of being poor – he made such efforts to be entertaining. When his story was concluded, there was much laughter and approbation, particularly from two or three deputy aldermen, who had been asleep a greater part of the time. There was, however, one tall, dry-looking old gentleman with beetling eyebrows, who maintained a grave and rather severe face throughout, now and then folding his arms, inclining his head, and looking down upon the floor, as if turning a doubt over in his mind. He was one of your wary men, who never laugh but upon good grounds – when they have reason and the law on their side. When the mirth of the rest of the company had subsided and silence was restored, he leaned one arm on the elbow of his chair, and, sticking the other akimbo, demanded, with a slight but exceedingly sage motion of the head, and contraction of the brow, what was the moral of the story, and what it went to prove?

The storyteller, who was just putting a glass of wine to his lips as a refreshment after his toils, paused for a moment, looked at his inquirer with an air of infinite deference, and, lowering the glass slowly to the table, observed that the story was intended most logically to prove:

'That there is no situation in life but has its advantages and pleasures – provided we will but take a joke as we find it.

'That, therefore, he that runs races with goblin troopers is likely to have rough riding of it.

'Ergo, for a country schoolmaster to be refused the hand of a Dutch heiress is a certain step to high preferment in the state.'

The cautious old gentleman knit his brows tenfold closer after this explanation, being sorely puzzled by the ratiocination of the syllogism; while, methought, the one in pepper-and-salt eyed him with something of a triumphant leer. At length, he observed, that all this was very well, but still he thought the story a little on the extravagant – there were one or two points on which he had his doubts.

'Faith, sir,' replied the storyteller, 'as to that matter, I don't believe one-half of it myself.'

D.K.

THE SPECTRE BRIDEGROOM

A TRAVELLER'S TALE

He that supper for is dight,
He lyes full cold, I trow, this night!
Yestreen to chamber I him led,
This night Gray-Steel has made his bed.

SIR EGER, SIR GRAHAME,
AND SIR GRAY-STEEL

On the summit of one of the heights of the Odenwald, a wild and romantic tract of Upper Germany that lies not far from the confluence of the Main and the Rhine, there stood, many, many years since, the Castle of the Baron Von Land-short. It is now quite fallen to decay and almost buried among beech trees and dark firs, above which, however, its old watchtower may still be seen, struggling, like the former possessor I have mentioned, to carry a high head and look down upon the neighbouring country.

The baron was a dry branch of the great family of Katzenellenbogen,* and inherited the relics of the property and all the pride of his ancestors. Though the warlike disposition of his predecessors had much impaired the family possessions, yet the baron still endeavoured to keep up some show of former state. The times were peaceable, and the German nobles, in general, had abandoned their inconvenient old castles, perched like eagles' nests among the mountains, and had built more convenient residences in the valleys; still the baron remained proudly drawn up in his little fortress, cherishing, with hereditary inveteracy, all the old family feuds, so that he was on ill terms with some of his nearest neighbours on account of disputes that had happened between their great-great-grandfathers.

The baron had but one child, a daughter; but nature, when she grants but one child, always compensates by making it a prodigy, and so it was with the daughter of the baron. All the nurses, gossips, and country cousins assured her father that she had not her equal for beauty in all Germany; and who should know better than they? She had, moreover, been brought up with great care under the superintendence of two maiden aunts, who had spent some years of their early life at one of the little German courts and were skilled in all the branches of knowledge necessary to the

* i.e. Cat's-elbow. The name of a family of those parts very powerful in former times. The appellation, we are told, was given in compliment to a peerless dame of the family, celebrated for her fine arm.

education of a fine lady. Under their instructions
she became a miracle of accomplishments. By the
time she was eighteen she could embroider to
admiration and had worked whole histories of the
saints in tapestry with such strength of expression
in their countenances that they looked like so
many souls in purgatory. She could read without
great difficulty, and had spelled her way through
several church legends and almost all the chivalric
wonders of the Heldenbuch. She had even made
considerable proficiency in writing, could sign her
own name without missing a letter, and so legibly
that her aunts could read it without spectacles.
She excelled in making little elegant good-for-noth-
ing ladylike knick-knacks of all kinds; was versed
in the most abstruse dancing of the day; played a
number of airs on the harp and guitar; and knew
all the tender ballads of the Minnelieders by
heart.

Her aunts, too, having been great flirts and
coquettes in their younger days, were admirably
calculated to be vigilant guardians and strict cen-
sors of the conduct of their niece, for there is no
chaperone so rigidly prudent and decorous as a
superannuated coquette. She was rarely suffered
out of their sight; never went beyond the domains
of the castle, unless well attended, or rather well
watched; had continual lectures read to her about
strict decorum and implicit obedience; and, as to
the men – pah! – she was taught to hold them at
such a distance, and in such absolute distrust,

that, unless properly authorized, she would not have cast a glance upon the handsomest cavalier in the world – no, not if he were even dying at her feet.

The good effects of this system were wonderfully apparent. The young lady was a pattern of docility and correctness. While others were wasting their sweetness in the glare of the world and liable to be plucked and thrown aside by every hand, she was coyly blooming into fresh and lovely womanhood under the protection of those immaculate spinsters, like a rosebud blushing forth among guardian thorns. Her aunts looked upon her with pride and exultation, and vaunted that though all the other young ladies in the world might go astray, yet, thank Heaven, nothing of the kind could happen to the heiress of Katzenellenbogen.

But, however scantily the Baron Von Landshort might be provided with children, his household was by no means a small one, for Providence had enriched him with abundance of poor relations. They, one and all, possessed the affectionate disposition common to humble relatives, were wonderfully attached to the baron, and took every possible occasion to come in swarms and enliven the castle. All family festivals were commemorated by these good people at the baron's expense; and when they were filled with good cheer they would declare that there was nothing on earth so delightful as these family meetings, these jubilees of the heart.

The baron, though a small man, had a large soul, and it swelled with satisfaction at the consciousness of being the greatest man in the little world about him. He loved to tell long stories about the dark old warriors whose portraits looked grimly down from the walls around, and he found no listeners equal to those that fed at his expense. He was much given to the marvellous, and a firm believer in all those supernatural tales with which every mountain and valley in Germany abounds. The faith of his guests exceeded even his own; they listened to every tale of wonder with open eyes and mouth, and never failed to be astonished, even though repeated for the hundredth time. Thus lived the Baron Von Landshort, the oracle of his table, the absolute monarch of his little territory, and happy, above all things, in the persuasion that he was the wisest man of the age.

At the time of which my story treats there was a great family gathering at the castle, on an affair of the utmost importance: it was to receive the destined bridegroom of the baron's daughter. A negotiation had been carried on between the father and an old nobleman of Bavaria to unite the dignity of their houses by the marriage of their children. The preliminaries had been conducted with proper punctilio. The young people were betrothed without seeing each other, and the time was appointed for the marriage ceremony. The young Count Von Altenburg had been recalled from the army for the purpose, and was actually on his way to the baron's to receive his bride. Missives had even been received from him, from Würzburg, where he was accidentally detained, mentioning the day and hour when he might be expected to arrive.

The castle was in a tumult of preparation to give him a suitable welcome. The fair bride had been decked out with uncommon care. The two aunts had superintended her toilet and quarrelled the whole morning about every article of her dress. The young lady had taken advantage of their contest to follow the bent of her own taste, and fortunately it was a good one. She looked as lovely as youthful bridegroom could desire, and the flutter of expectation heightened the lustre of her charms.

The suffusions that mantled her face and neck, the gentle heaving of the bosom, the eye now and then lost in reverie, all betrayed the soft tumult that was going on in her little heart. The aunts were continually hovering around her, for maiden aunts are apt to take great interest in affairs of this nature. They were giving her a world of staid counsel how to deport herself, what to say, and in what manner to receive the expected lover.

The baron was no less busied in preparations. He had, in truth, nothing exactly to do, but he was naturally a fuming bustling little man, and could not remain passive when all the world was in a hurry. He worried from top to bottom of the castle with an air of infinite anxiety; he continually called the servants from their work to exhort them to be diligent; and buzzed about every hall and chamber, as idly restless and importunate as a bluebottle fly on a warm summer's day.

In the meantime the fatted calf had been killed; the forests had rung with the clamour of the huntsmen; the kitchen was crowded with good cheer; the cellars had yielded up whole oceans of *Rhein-wein* and *Ferne-wein*; and even the great Heidelberg tun had been laid under contribution. Everything was ready to receive the distinguished guest with *Saus und Braus* in the true spirit of German hospitality – but the guest delayed to make his appearance. Hour rolled after hour. The sun that had poured his downward rays upon the rich forest of the Odenwald now just gleamed along the summits of the mountains. The baron mounted the highest tower, and strained his eyes in hope of catching a distant sight of the count and his attendants. Once he thought he beheld them; the sound of horns came floating from the valley, prolonged by the mountain echoes. A number of horsemen were seen far below, slowly advancing along the road; but when they had nearly reached the foot of the mountain they suddenly struck off in a different direction. The last ray of sunshine departed – the bats began to flit by in the twilight – the road grew dimmer and dimmer to the view; and nothing appeared stirring in it but now and then a peasant lagging homeward from his labour.

While the old castle of Landshort was in this state of perplexity a very interesting scene was transacting in a different part of the Odenwald.

The young Count Von Altenburg was tranquilly pursuing his route in that sober jog-trot way, in which a man travels toward matrimony when his friends have taken all the trouble and uncertainty of courtship off his hands, and a bride is waiting for him as certainly as a dinner at the end of his journey. He had encountered at Würzburg a youthful companion in arms with whom he had seen some service on the frontiers, Herman Von Starkenfaust, one of the stoutest hands and worthiest hearts of German chivalry, who was now returning from the army. His father's castle was not far distant from the old fortress of Landshort, although an hereditary feud rendered the families hostile and strangers to each other.

In the warmhearted moment of recognition the young friends related all their past adventures and fortunes, and the count gave the whole history of his intended nuptials with a young lady whom he had never seen but of whose charms he had received the most enrapturing descriptions.

As the route of the friends lay in the same direction, they agreed to perform the rest of their journey together; and, that they might do it the more leisurely, set off from Würzburg at an early hour, the count having given directions for his retinue to follow and overtake him.

They beguiled their wayfaring with recollections of their military scenes and adventures; but the count was apt to be a little tedious, now and then, about the reputed charms of his bride, and the felicity that awaited him.

In this way they had entered among the mountains of the Odenwald, and were traversing one of its most lonely and thickly wooded passes. It is well known that the forests of Germany have always been as much infested by robbers as its castles by spectres; and at this time the former were particularly numerous, from the hordes of disbanded soldiers wandering about the country. It will not appear extraordinary, therefore, that the cavaliers were attacked by a gang of these stragglers in the midst of the forest. They defended themselves with bravery, but were nearly overpowered, when the count's retinue arrived to their assistance. At sight of them the robbers fled, but not until the count had received a mortal wound. He was slowly and carefully conveyed back to the city of Würzburg, and a friar summoned from a neighbouring convent, who was famous for his skill in administering to both soul and body; but half of his skill was superfluous; the moments of the unfortunate count were numbered.

With his dying breath he entreated his friend to repair instantly to the castle of Landshort and explain the fatal cause of his not keeping his appointment with his bride. Though not the most ardent of lovers, he was one of the most punctilious of men, and appeared earnestly solicitous that his mission should be speedily and courteously executed. 'Unless this is done,' said he, 'I shall not sleep quietly in my grave!' He repeated these last words with peculiar solemnity. A request, at a moment so impressive, admitted no hesitation. Starkenfaust endeavoured to soothe him to calmness, promised faithfully to execute his wish, and gave him his hand in solemn pledge. The dying man pressed it in acknowledgement, but soon lapsed into delirium – raved about his bride – his engagements – his plighted word; ordered his horse that he might ride to the castle of Landshort; and expired in the fancied act of vaulting into the saddle.

Starkenfaust bestowed a sigh and a soldier's tear on the untimely fate of his comrade, and then pondered on the awkward mission he had undertaken. His heart was heavy and his head perplexed, for he was to present himself an unbidden guest among hostile people, and to damp their festivity with tidings fatal to their hopes. Still there were certain whisperings of curiosity in his bosom to see this far-famed beauty of Katzenellenbogen, so cautiously shut up from the world, for he was a passionate admirer of the sex, and there was a dash of eccentricity and enterprise in his character that made him fond of all singular adventure.

Previous to his departure he made all due arrangements with the holy fraternity of the convent for the funeral solemnities of his friend, who was to be buried in the cathedral of Würzburg, near some of his illustrious relatives; and the mourning retinue of the count took charge of his remains.

It is now high time that we should return to the ancient family of Katzenellenbogen, who were impatient for their guest, and still more for their dinner; and to the worthy little baron, whom we left airing himself on the watchtower.

Night closed in, but still no guest arrived. The baron descended from the tower in despair. The banquet, which had been delayed from hour to hour, could no longer be postponed. The meats were already overdone; the cook in an agony; and the whole household had the look of a garrison that had been reduced by famine. The baron was obliged reluctantly to give orders for the feast without the presence of the guest. All were seated at table, and just on the point of commencing when the sound of a horn from without the gate gave notice of the approach of a stranger. Another long blast filled the old courts of the castle with its echoes, and was answered by the warder from the walls. The baron hastened to receive his future son-in-law.

The drawbridge had been let down, and the stranger was before the gate. He was a tall, gallant cavalier, mounted on a black steed. His countenance was pale, but he had a beaming, romantic eye, and an air of stately melancholy. The baron was a little mortified that he should have come in this simple, solitary style. His dignity for a moment was ruffled, and he felt disposed to consider it a want of proper respect for the important occasion and the important family with which he was to be connected. He pacified himself, however, with the conclusion that it must have been youthful impatience which had induced him thus to spur on sooner than his attendants.

'I am sorry,' said the stranger, 'to break in upon you thus unseasonably –'

Here the baron interrupted him with a world of compliments and greetings, for, to tell the truth, he prided himself upon his courtesy and eloquence. The stranger attempted, once or twice, to stem the torrent of words, but in vain, so he bowed his head and suffered it to flow on. By the time the baron had come to a pause, they had reached the inner court of the castle, and the stranger was again about to speak when he was once more interrupted by the appearance of the female part of the family, leading forth the shrinking and blushing bride. He gazed on her for a moment as one entranced; it seemed as if his whole soul beamed forth in the gaze, and rested upon that lovely form. One of the maiden aunts whispered something in her ear; she made an effort to speak; her moist blue eye was timidly raised, gave a shy glance of inquiry on the stranger, and was cast again to the ground. The words died away, but there was a sweet smile playing about her lips and a soft dimpling of the cheek that showed her glance had not been unsatisfactory. It was impossible for a girl of the fond age of eighteen, highly predisposed for love and matrimony, not to be pleased with so gallant a cavalier.

The late hour at which the guest had arrived left no time for parley. The baron was peremptory, and deferred all particular conversation until the morning, and led the way to the untasted banquet.

It was served up in the great hall of the castle. Around the walls hung the hard-favoured portraits of the heroes of the house of Katzenellenbogen and the trophies which they had gained in the field and the chase. Hacked corslets, splintered jousting spears, and tattered banners were mingled with the spoils of sylvan warfare; the jaws of the wolf and the tusks of the boar grinned horribly among cross-bows and battle-axes, and a huge pair of antlers branched immediately over the head of the youthful bridegroom.

The cavalier took but little notice of the company or the entertainment. He scarcely tasted the banquet, but seemed absorbed in admiration of his bride. He conversed in a low tone that could not be overheard – for the language of love is never loud; but where is the female ear so dull that it cannot catch the softest whisper of the lover? There was a mingled tenderness and gravity in his manner that appeared to have a powerful effect upon the young lady. Her colour came and went as she listened with deep attention. Now and then she made some blushing reply, and when his eye was turned away, she would steal a sidelong glance at his romantic countenance and heave a gentle sigh of tender happiness. It was evident that the young couple were completely enamoured. The aunts, who were deeply versed in the mysteries of the heart, declared that they had fallen in love with each other at first sight.

The feast went on merrily, or at least noisily, for the guests were all blessed with those keen appetites that attend upon light purses and mountain air. The baron told his best and longest stories, and never had he told them so well or with such great effect. If there was anything marvellous, his auditors were lost in astonishment; and if anything facetious, they were sure to laugh exactly in the right place. The baron, it is true, like most great men, was too dignified to utter any joke but a dull one; it was always enforced, however, by a bumper of excellent Hockheimer, and even a dull joke, at one's own table, served up with jolly old wine, is irresistible. Many good things were said by poorer and keener wits that would not bear repeating, except on similar occasions; many sly speeches whispered in ladies' ears that almost convulsed them with suppressed laughter; and a song or two roared out by a poor but merry and broad-faced cousin of the baron that absolutely made the maiden aunts hold up their fans.

Amidst all this revelry, the stranger guest maintained a most singular and unseasonable gravity.

His countenance assumed a deeper cast of dejection as the evening advanced; and, strange as it may appear, even the baron's jokes seemed only to render him the more melancholy. At times he was lost in thought, and at times there was a perturbed and restless wandering of the eye that bespoke a mind but ill at ease. His conversations with the bride became more and more earnest and mysterious. Lowering clouds began to steal over the fair serenity of her brow, and tremors to run through her tender frame.

All this could not escape the notice of the company. Their gaiety was chilled by the unaccountable gloom of the bridegroom; their spirits were infected; whispers and glances were interchanged, accompanied by shrugs and dubious shakes of the head. The song and the laugh grew less and less frequent; there were dreary pauses in the conversation, which were at length succeeded by wild tales and supernatural legends. One dismal story produced another still more dismal, and the baron nearly frightened some of the ladies into hysterics with the history of the goblin horseman that carried away the fair Leonora; a dreadful story, which has since been put into excellent verse, and is read and believed by all the world.

The bridegroom listened to this tale with profound attention. He kept his eyes steadily fixed on the baron, and, as the story drew to a close, began gradually to rise from his seat, growing taller and taller, until, in the baron's entranced eye, he seemed almost to tower into a giant. The moment the tale was finished, he heaved a sigh, and took a solemn farewell of the company. They were all amazement. The baron was perfectly thunder-struck.

'What! Going to leave the castle at midnight? Why, everything was prepared for his reception; a chamber was ready for him if he wished to retire.'

The stranger shook his head mournfully and mysteriously. 'I must lay my head in a different chamber tonight!'

There was something in this reply and the tone in which it was uttered that made the baron's heart misgive him, but he rallied his forces and repeated his hospitable entreaties.

The stranger shook his head silently, but positively, at every offer; and, waving his farewell to the company, stalked slowly out of the hall. The maiden aunts were absolutely petrified – the bride hung her head, and a tear stole to her eye.

The baron followed the stranger to the great court of the castle, where the black charger stood pawing the earth, and snorting with impatience. When they had reached the portal, whose deep archway was dimly lighted by a cresset, the stranger paused, and addressed the baron in a hollow tone of voice, which the vaulted roof rendered still more sepulchral.

'Now that we are alone,' said he, 'I will impart to you the reason of my going. I have a solemn, an indispensable engagement –'

'Why,' said the baron, 'cannot you send some-one in your place?'

'It admits of no substitute – I must attend it in person – I must away to Würzburg cathedral –'

'Ay,' said the baron, plucking up spirit, 'but not until tomorrow – tomorrow you shall take your bride there.'

'No! no!' replied the stranger, with tenfold solemnity, 'my engagement is with no bride – the worms! The worms expect me! I am a dead man – I have been slain by robbers – my body lies at Würzburg – at midnight I am to be buried – the grave is waiting for me – I must keep my appointment!'

He sprang on his black charger, dashed over the drawbridge, and the clattering of his horse's hoofs was lost in the whistling of the night blast.

The baron returned to the hall in the utmost consternation and related what had passed. Two ladies fainted outright, others sickened at the idea of having banqueted with a spectre. It was the opinion of some that this might be the wild huntsman, famous in German legend. Some talked of mountain sprites, of wood demons, and of other supernatural beings, with which the good. people of Germany have been so grievously harassed since time immemorial. One of the poor relations ventured to suggest that it might be some sportive evasion of the young cavalier, and that the very gloominess of the caprice seemed to accord with so melancholy a personage. This, however, drew on him the indignation of the whole company, and especially of the baron, who looked upon him as little better than an infidel, so that he was fain to abjure his heresy as speedily as possible and come into the faith of the true believers.

But whatever may have been the doubts entertained, they were completely put to an end by the arrival, next day, of regular missives, confirming the intelligence of the young count's murder, and his interment in Würzburg cathedral.

The dismay at the castle may well be imagined. The baron shut himself up in his chamber. The guests, who had come to rejoice with him, could not think of abandoning him in his distress. They wandered about the courts, or collected in groups in the hall, shaking their heads and shrugging their shoulders at the troubles of so good a man; and sat longer than ever at table, and ate and drank more stoutly than ever, by way of keeping up their spirits. But the situation of the widowed bride was the most pitiable. To have lost a husband before she had even embraced him – and such a husband! If the very spectre could be so gracious and noble, what must have been the living man? She filled the house with lamentations.

On the night of the second day of her widowhood, she had retired to her chamber, accompanied by one of her aunts, who insisted on sleeping with her. The aunt, who was one of the best tellers of ghost stories in all Germany, had just been recounting one of her longest, and had fallen asleep in the very midst of it. The chamber was remote, and overlooked a small garden. The niece lay pensively gazing at the beams of the rising moon, as they trembled on the leaves of an aspen tree before the lattice. The castle clock had just tolled midnight when a soft strain of music stole up from the garden. She rose hastily from her bed, and stepped lightly to the window. A tall figure stood among the shadows of the trees. As it raised its head, a beam of moonlight fell upon the countenance. Heaven and earth! She beheld the Spectre Bridegroom! A loud shriek at that moment burst upon her ear, and her aunt, who had been awakened by the music and had followed her silently to the window, fell into her arms. When she looked again, the spectre had disappeared.

Of the two females, the aunt now required the more soothing, for she was perfectly beside herself with terror. As to the young lady, there was something, even in the spectre of her lover, that seemed endearing. There was still the semblance of manly beauty; and though the shadow of a man is but little calculated to satisfy the affections of a love-sick girl, yet, where the substance is not to be had, even that is consoling. The aunt declared she would never sleep in that chamber again; the niece, for once, was refractory, and declared as strongly that she would sleep in no other in the castle. The consequence was that she had to sleep in it alone; but she drew a promise from her aunt not to relate the story of the spectre, lest she should be denied the only melancholy pleasure left her on earth – that of inhabiting the chamber over which the guardian shade of her lover kept its nightly vigils.

How long the good old lady would have observed this promise is uncertain, for she dearly loved to talk of the marvellous, and there is a triumph in being the first to tell a frightful story; it is, however, still quoted in the neighbourhood, as a memorable instance of female secrecy, that she kept it to herself for a whole week, when she was suddenly absolved from all further restraint by intelligence brought to the breakfast table one morning that the young lady was not to be found. Her room was empty – the bed had not been slept in – the window was open, and the bird had flown!

The astonishment and concern with which the intelligence was received can only be imagined by those who have witnessed the agitation which the mishaps of a great man cause among his friends. Even the poor relations paused for a moment from the indefatigable labours of the trencher, when the aunt, who had at first been struck speechless, wrung her hands, and shrieked out, 'The goblin! The goblin! She's carried away by the goblin.'

In a few words she related the fearful scene of the garden, and concluded that the spectre must have carried off his bride. Two of the domestics corroborated the opinion, for they had heard the clattering of a horse's hoofs down the mountain about midnight, and had no doubt that it was the spectre on his black charger, bearing her away to the tomb. All present were struck with the direful probability, for events of the kind are extremely common in Germany, as many well-authenticated histories bear witness.

What a lamentable situation was that of the poor baron! What a heart-rending dilemma for a fond father, and a member of the great family of Katzenellenbogen! His only daughter had either been rapt away to the grave, or he was to have some wood demon for a son-in-law, and, perchance, a troop of goblin grandchildren. As usual, he was completely bewildered, and all the castle in an uproar. The men were ordered to take horse and scour every road and path and glen of the Odenwald. The baron himself had just drawn on his jack boots, girded on his sword, and was about to mount his steed to sally forth on the doubtful quest when he was brought to a pause by a new apparition. A lady was seen approaching the castle, mounted on a palfrey, attended by a cavalier on horseback. She galloped up to the gate, sprang from her horse, and, falling at the baron's feet, embraced his knees. It was his lost daughter and her companion – the Spectre Bridegroom! The baron was astounded. He looked at his daughter, then at the spectre, and almost doubted the evidence of his senses. The latter, too, was wonderfully improved in his appearance since his visit to the world of spirits. His dress was splendid, and set off a noble figure of manly symmetry. He was no longer pale and melancholy. His fine countenance was flushed with the glow of youth, and joy rioted in his large dark eye.

The mystery was soon cleared up. The cavalier (for, in truth, as you must have known all the while, he was no goblin) announced himself as Sir Herman Von Starkenfaust. He related his adventure with the young count. He told how he had hastened to the castle to deliver the unwelcome tidings, but that the eloquence of the baron had interrupted him in every attempt to tell his tale. How the sight of the bride had completely captivated him, and that to pass a few hours near her he had tacitly suffered the mistake to continue. How he had been sorely perplexed in what way to make a decent retreat, until the baron's goblin stories had suggested his eccentric exit. How, fearing the feudal hostility of the family, he had repeated his visits by stealth – had haunted the garden beneath the young lady's window – had wooed – had won – had borne away in triumph – and, in a word, had wedded the fair.

Under any other circumstances the baron would have been inflexible, for he was tenacious of paternal authority and devoutly obstinate in all family feuds; but he loved his daughter; he had lamented her as lost; he rejoiced to find her still alive; and, though her husband was of a hostile house, yet, thank Heaven, he was not a goblin. There was something, it must be acknowledged, that did not exactly accord with his notions of strict veracity, in the joke the knight had passed upon him of his being a dead man; but several old friends present, who had served in the wars, assured him that every stratagem was excusable in love, and that the cavalier was entitled to especial privilege, having lately served as a trooper.

Matters, therefore, were happily arranged. The baron pardoned the young couple on the spot. The revels at the castle were resumed. The poor relations overwhelmed this new member of the family with loving kindness; he was so gallant, so generous – and so rich. The aunts, it is true, were somewhat scandalized that their system of strict seclusion and passive obedience should be so badly exemplified, but attributed it all to their negligence in not having the windows grated. One of them was particularly mortified at having her marvellous story marred, and that the only spectre she had ever seen should turn out a counterfeit but the niece seemed perfectly happy at having found him substantial flesh and blood – and so the story ends.

THE PRIDE OF THE VILLAGE

May no wolfe howle; no screech owle stir
A wing about thy sepulchre!
No boysterous winds or stormes come hither,
　　　To starve or wither
Thy soft sweet earth! but, like a spring,
Love kept it ever flourishing.

HERRICK

In the course of an excursion through one of the remote counties of England, I had struck into one of those crossroads that lead through the more secluded parts of the country, and stopped one afternoon at a village, the situation of which was beautifully rural and retired. There was an air of primitive simplicity about its inhabitants, not to be found in the villages which lie on the great coach roads. I determined to pass the night there, and, having taken an early dinner, strolled out to enjoy the neighbouring scenery.

My ramble, as is usually the case with travellers, soon led me to the church, which stood at a little distance from the village. Indeed, it was an object of some curiosity, its old tower being completely

overrun with ivy, so that only here and there a
jutting buttress, an angle of grey wall, or a fantasti-
cally carved ornament peered through the verdant
covering. It was a lovely evening. The early part
of the day had been dark and showery, but in the
afternoon it had cleared up; and though sullen
clouds still hung overhead, yet there was a broad
tract of golden sky in the west from which the
setting sun gleamed through the dripping leaves,
and lit up all nature with a melancholy smile. It
seemed like the parting hour of a good Christian,
smiling on the sins and sorrows of the world, and
giving, in the serenity of his decline, an assurance
that he will rise again in glory.

I had seated myself on a half-sunken tombstone,
and was musing, as one is apt to do at this sober-
thoughted hour, on past scenes and early friends –
on those who were distant and those who were
dead – and indulging in that kind of melancholy
fancying which has in it something sweeter even
than pleasure. Every now and then the stroke of a
bell from the neighbouring tower fell on my ear;
its tones were in unison with the scene, and,
instead of jarring, chimed in with my feelings,
and it was some time before I recollected that it
must be tolling the knell of some new tenant of
the tomb.

Presently I saw a funeral train moving across
the village green; it wound slowly along a lane,
was lost, and reappeared through the breaks of
the hedges, until it passed the place where I was

sitting. The pall was supported by young girls, dressed in white; and another, about the age of seventeen, walked before, bearing a chaplet of white flowers, a token that the deceased was a young and unmarried female. The corpse was followed by the parents. They were a venerable couple of the better order of peasantry. The father seemed to repress his feelings, but his fixed eye, contracted brow, and deeply-furrowed face showed the struggle that was passing within. His wife hung on his arm, and wept aloud with the convulsive bursts of a mother's sorrow.

I followed the funeral into the church. The bier was placed in the centre aisle, and the chaplet of white flowers, with a pair of white gloves, were hung over the seat which the deceased had occupied.

Everyone knows the soul-subduing pathos of the funeral service, for who is so fortunate as never to have followed someone he has loved to the tomb? But when performed over the remains of innocence and beauty, thus laid low in the bloom of existence – what can be more affecting? At that simple but most solemn consignment of the body to the grave – 'Earth to earth – ashes to ashes – dust to dust!' – the tears of the youthful companions of the deceased flowed unrestrained. The father still seemed to struggle with his feelings, and to comfort himself with the assurance that the dead are blessed which die in the Lord; but the mother only thought of her child as a

flower of the field cut down and withered in the
midst of its sweetness; she was like Rachel, 'mourning over her children, and would not be
comforted'.

On returning to the inn, I learned the whole
story of the deceased. It was a simple one, and
such as has often been told. She had been the
beauty and pride of the village. Her father had
once been an opulent farmer, but was reduced in
circumstances. This was an only child, and
brought up entirely at home, in the simplicity of
rural life. She had been the pupil of the village
pastor, the favourite lamb of his little flock. The
good man watched over her education with paternal care; it was limited, and suitable to the sphere
in which she was to move, for he only sought to
make her an ornament to her station in life, not to
raise her above it. The tenderness and indulgence
of her parents and the exemption from all ordinary
occupations had fostered a natural grace and delicacy of character that accorded with the fragile
loveliness of her form. She appeared like some
tender plant of the garden, blooming accidentally
amid the hardier natives of the fields.

The superiority of her charms was felt and
acknowledged by her companions, but without
envy, for it was surpassed by the unassuming
gentleness and winning kindness of her manners.
It might be truly said of her:

This is the prettiest low-born lass, that ever

Ran on the green-sward; nothing she does or
    seems,
But smacks of something greater than herself;
Too noble for this place.

The village was one of those sequestered spots
which still retain some vestiges of old English
customs. It had its rural festivals and holiday
pastimes, and still kept up some faint observance
of the once-popular rites of May. These, indeed,
had been promoted by its present pastor, who was
a lover of old customs and one of those simple
Christians that think their mission fulfilled by
promoting joy on earth and good will among mankind. Under his auspices the Maypole stood from
year to year in the centre of the village green; on
May Day it was decorated with garlands and
streamers, and a queen or lady of the May was
appointed, as in former times, to preside at the
sports and distribute the prizes and rewards. The
picturesque situation of the village and the fanciful-
ness of its rustic fetes would often attract the
notice of casual visitors. Among these, on one
May Day, was a young officer whose regiment
had been recently quartered in the neighbourhood. He was charmed with the native taste that
pervaded this village pageant, but, above all, with
the dawning loveliness of the queen of May. It
was the village favourite, who was crowned with
flowers, and blushing and smiling in all the beautiful confusion of girlish diffidence and delight.

The artlessness of rural habits enabled him readily
to make her acquaintance; he gradually won his
way into her intimacy; and paid his court to her in
that unthinking way in which young officers are
too apt to trifle with rustic simplicity.

There was nothing in his advances to startle or
alarm. He never even talked of love; but there are
modes of making it more eloquent than language,
and which convey it subtilely and irresistibly to
the heart. The beam of the eye, the tone of voice,
the thousand tendernesses which emanate from
every word and look and action – these form the
true eloquence of love, and can always be felt and
understood, but never described. Can we wonder
that they should readily win a heart, young, guileless, and susceptible? As to her, she loved almost
unconsciously; she scarcely inquired what was the
growing passion that was absorbing every thought
and feeling, or what were to be its consequences.
She, indeed, looked not to the future. When
present, his looks and words occupied her whole
attention; when absent, she thought but of what
had passed at their recent interview. She would
wander with him through the green lanes and
rural scenes of the vicinity. He taught her to see
new beauties in nature; he talked in the language
of polite and cultivated life, and breathed into her
ear the witcheries of romance and poetry.

Perhaps there could not have been a passion
between the sexes more pure than this innocent
girl's. The gallant figure of her youthful admirer

and the splendour of his military attire might at first have charmed her eye; but it was not these that had captivated her heart. Her attachment had something in it of idolatry. She looked up to him as to a being of a superior order. She felt in his society the enthusiasm of a mind naturally delicate and poetical, and now first awakened to a keen perception of the beautiful and grand. Of the sordid distinctions of rank and fortune she thought nothing; it was the difference of intellect, of demeanour, of manners from those of the rustic society to which she had been accustomed that elevated him in her opinion. She would listen to him with charmed ear and downcast look of mute delight, and her cheek would mantle with enthusiasm; or if ever she ventured a shy glance of timid admiration, it was as quickly withdrawn, and she would sigh and blush at the idea of her comparative unworthiness.

Her lover was equally impassioned; but his passion was mingled with feelings of a coarser nature. He had begun the connection in levity, for he had often heard his brother officers boast of their village conquests, and thought some triumph of the kind necessary to his reputation as a man of spirit. But he was too full of youthful fervour. His heart had not yet been rendered sufficiently cold and selfish by a wandering and a dissipated life; it caught fire from the very flame it sought to kindle, and before he was aware of the nature of his situation he became really in love.

What was he to do? There were the old obstacles which so incessantly occur in these heedless attachments. His rank in life – the prejudices of titled connections – his dependence upon a proud and unyielding father – all forbade him to think of matrimony: but when he looked down upon this innocent being, so tender and confiding, there was a purity in her manners, a blamelessness in her life, and a beseeching modesty in her looks that awed down every licentious feeling. In vain did he try to fortify himself by a thousand heartless examples of men of fashion, and to chill the glow of generous sentiment with that cold derisive levity with which he had heard them talk of female virtue; whenever he came into her presence, she was still surrounded by that mysterious but impassive charm of virgin purity in whose hallowed sphere no guilty thought can live.

The sudden arrival of orders for the regiment to repair to the continent completed the confusion of his mind. He remained for a short time in a state of the most painful irresolution; he hesitated to communicate the tidings until the day for marching was at hand, when he gave her the intelligence in the course of an evening ramble.

The idea of parting had never before occurred to her. It broke in at once upon her dream of felicity; she looked upon it as a sudden and insurmountable evil, and wept with the guileless simplicity of a child. He drew her to his bosom, and kissed the tears from her soft cheek; nor did he meet with a repulse, for there are moments of mingled sorrow and tenderness which hallow the caresses of affection. He was naturally impetuous; and the sight of beauty, apparently yielding in his arms, the confidence of his power over her, and the dread of losing her for ever, all conspired to overwhelm his better feelings – he ventured to propose that she should leave her home and be the companion of his fortunes.

He was quite a novice in seduction, and blushed and faltered at his own baseness; but so innocent of mind was his intended victim that she was at first at a loss to comprehend his meaning; and why she should leave her native village, and the humble roof of her parents. When at last the nature of his proposal flashed upon her pure mind, the effect was withering. She did not weep – she did not break forth into reproach – she said not a word – but she shrunk back aghast as from a viper; gave him a look of anguish that pierced to his very soul; and, clasping her hands in agony, fled, as if for refuge, to her father's cottage.

The officer retired, confounded, humiliated, and repentant. It is uncertain what might have been the result of the conflict of his feelings had not his thoughts been diverted by the bustle of departure. New scenes, new pleasures, and new companions soon dissipated his self-reproach and stifled his tenderness; yet, amidst the stir of camps, the revelries of garrisons, the array of armies, and even the din of battles, his thoughts would sometimes steal back to the scenes of rural quiet and village simplicity – the white cottage – the footpath along the silver brook and up the hawthorn hedge, and the little village maid loitering along it, leaning on his arm, and listening to him with eyes beaming with unconscious affection.

The shock which the poor girl had received, in the destruction of all her ideal world, had indeed been cruel. Faintings and hysterics had at first shaken her tender frame, and were succeeded by a settled and pining melancholy. She had beheld from her window the march of the departing troops. She had seen her faithless lover borne off, as if in triumph, amidst the sound of drum and trumpet and the pomp of arms. She strained a last aching gaze after him, as the morning sun glittered about his figure, and his plume waved in the breeze; he passed away like a bright vision from her sight, and left her all in darkness.

It would be trite to dwell on the particulars of her after story. It was, like other tales of love, melancholy. She avoided society, and wandered out alone in the walks she had most frequented with her lover. She sought, like the stricken deer, to weep in silence and loneliness, and brood over the barbed sorrow that rankled in her soul. Sometimes she would be seen late of an evening sitting in the porch of the village church; and the milkmaids, returning from the fields, would now and then overhear her singing some plaintive ditty in the hawthorn walk. She became fervent in her devotions at church; and as the old people saw her approach, so wasted away, yet with a hectic bloom, and that hallowed air which melancholy diffuses around the form, they would make way for her, as for something spiritual, and, looking after her, would shake their heads in gloomy foreboding.

She felt a conviction that she was hastening to the tomb, but looked forward to it as a place of rest. The silver cord that had bound her to existence was loosed, and there seemed to be no more pleasure under the sun. If ever her gentle bosom had entertained resentment against her lover, it was extinguished. She was incapable of angry passions; and in a moment of saddened tenderness, she penned him a farewell letter. It was couched in the simplest language, but touching from its very simplicity. She told him that she was dying, and did not conceal from him that his conduct was the cause. She even depicted the sufferings which she had experienced, but concluded with saying that she could not die in peace until she had sent him her forgiveness and her blessing.

By degrees her strength declined, that she could no longer leave the cottage. She could only totter to the window, where, propped up in her chair, it was her enjoyment to sit all day and look out upon the landscape. Still she uttered no complaint, nor imparted to anyone the malady that was preying on her heart. She never even mentioned her lover's name, but would lay her head on her mother's bosom and weep in silence. Her poor parents hung, in mute anxiety, over this fading blossom of their hopes, still flattering themselves that it might again revive to freshness, and that the bright unearthly bloom which sometimes flushed her cheek might be the promise of returning health.

In this way she was seated between them one Sunday afternoon; her hands were clasped in theirs, the lattice was thrown open, and the soft air that stole in brought with it the fragrance of the clustering honeysuckle which her own hands had trained around the window.

Her father had just been reading a chapter in the Bible; it spoke of the vanity of worldly things, and of the joys of heaven; it seemed to have diffused comfort and serenity through her bosom. Her eye was fixed on the distant village church; the bell had tolled for the evening service; the last villager was lagging into the porch; and everything had sunk into that hallowed stillness peculiar to the day of rest. Her parents were gazing on her with yearning hearts. Sickness and sorrow, which pass so roughly over some faces, had given to hers the expression of a seraph's. A tear trembled in her soft blue eye. Was she thinking of her faithless lover? Or were her thoughts wandering to that distant churchyard, into whose bosom she might soon be gathered?

Suddenly the clang of hoofs was heard – a horseman galloped to the cottage – he dismounted before the window – the poor girl gave a faint exclamation, and sank back in her chair: it was her repentant lover! He rushed into the house and flew to clasp her to his bosom; but her wasted form – her deathlike countenance – so wan, yet so lovely in its desolation – smote him to the soul, and he threw himself in agony at her feet. She was too faint to rise – she attempted to extend her trembling hand – her lips moved as if she spoke, but no word was articulated – she looked down upon him with a smile of unutterable tenderness – and closed her eyes for ever!

Such are the particulars which I gathered of this village story. They are but scanty, and I am conscious have little novelty to recommend them. In the present rage also for strange incident and high-seasoned narrative they may appear trite and insignificant, but they interested me strongly at the time; and, taken in connection with the affecting ceremony which I had just witnessed, left a deeper impression on my mind than many circumstances of a more striking nature. I have passed through the place since, and visited the church again, from a better motive than mere curiosity. It was a wintry evening; the trees were stripped of their foliage; the churchyard looked naked and mournful, and the wind rustled coldly through the dry grass. Evergreens, however, had been planted about the grave of the village favourite, and osiers were bent over it to keep the turf uninjured.

The church door was open, and I stepped in.

There hung the chaplet of flowers and the gloves, as on the day of the funeral; the flowers were withered, it is true, but care seemed to have been taken that no dust should soil their whiteness. I have seen many monuments where art has exhausted its powers to awaken the sympathy of the spectator, but I have met with none that spoke more touchingly to my heart than this simple but delicate memento of departed innocence.

MOUNTJOY

OR SOME PASSAGES OUT OF THE LIFE OF A CASTLE-BUILDER

I was born among romantic scenery, in one of the wildest parts of the Hudson, which at that time was not so thickly settled as at present. My father was descended from one of the old Huguenot families, that came over to this country on the revocation of the edict of Nantes. He lived in a style of easy, rural independence, on a patrimonial estate that had been for two or three generations in the family. He was an indolent, good-natured man, who took the world as it went, and had a kind of laughing philosophy, that parried all rubs and mishaps, and served him in the place of wisdom. This was the part of his character least to my taste; for I was of an enthusiastic, excitable temperament, prone to kindle up with new schemes and projects, and he was apt to dash my sallying enthusiasm by some unlucky joke; so that whenever I was in a glow with any sudden excitement, I stood in mortal dread of his good-humour.

Yet he indulged me in every vagary for I was an only son, and of course a personage of importance in the household. I had two sisters older than myself, and one younger. The former were educated at New York, under the eye of a maiden aunt; the latter remained at home, and was my cherished playmate, the companion of my thoughts. We were two imaginative little beings, of quick susceptibility, and prone to see wonders and mysteries in everything around us. Scarce had we learned to read, when our mother made us holiday presents of all the nursery literature of the day; which at that time consisted of little books covered with gilt paper, adorned with 'cuts', and filled with tales of fairies, giants, and enchanters. What draughts of delightful fiction did we then inhale! My sister Sophy was of a soft and tender nature. She would weep over the woes of the Children in the Wood, or quake at the dark romance of Blue-Beard, and the terrible mysteries of the blue chamber. But I was all for enterprise and adventure. I burned to emulate the deeds of that heroic prince who delivered the white cat from her enchantment; or he of no less royal blood, and doughty emprise, who broke the charmed slumber of the Beauty in the Wood!

The house in which we lived was just the kind of place to foster such propensities. It was a venerable mansion, half villa, half farmhouse. The oldest part was of stone, with loop-holes for musketry, having served as a family fortress in the

time of the Indians. To this there had been made
various additions, some of brick, some of wood,
according to the exigencies of the moment; so that
it was full of nooks and crooks, and chambers of
all sorts and sizes. It was buried among willows,
elms, and cherry trees, and surrounded with roses
and hollyhocks with honeysuckle and sweet-briar
clambering about every window. A brood of hereditary pigeons sunned themselves upon the roof;
hereditary swallows and martins built about the
eaves and chimneys; and hereditary bees hummed
about the flower-beds.

Under the influence of our story-books every
object around us now assumed a new character,
and a charmed interest. The wild flowers were no
longer the mere ornaments of the fields, or the
resorts of the toilful bee; they were the lurking
places of fairies. We would watch the humming-
bird, as it hovered around the trumpet creeper at
our porch, and the butterfly as it flitted up into
the blue air, above the sunny tree tops, and fancy
them some of the tiny beings from fairyland. I
would call to mind all that I had read of Robin
Goodfellow and his power of transformation. Oh,
how I envied him that power! How I longed to be
able to compress my form into utter littleness; to
ride the bold dragon-fly; swing on the tall bearded
grass; follow the ant into his subterraneous habitation, or dive into the cavernous depths of the
honeysuckle!

While I was yet a mere child I was sent to a

daily school, about two miles distant. The school-house was on the edge of wood, close by a brook overhung with birches, alders, and dwarf willows. We of the school who lived at some distance came with our dinners put up in little baskets. In the intervals of school hours we would gather round a spring, under a tuft of hazel-bushes, and have a kind of picnic; interchanging the rustic dainties with which our provident mothers had fitted us out. Then when our joyous repast was over, and my companions were disposed for play, I would draw forth one of my cherished story-books, stretch myself on the greensward, and soon lose myself in its bewitching contents.

I became an oracle among my schoolmates on account of my superior erudition, and soon imparted to them the contagion of my infected fancy. Often in the evening, after school hours, we would sit on the trunk of some fallen tree in the woods, and vie with each other in telling extravagant stories, until the whippoor will began his nightly moaning, and the fire-flies sparkled in the gloom. Then came the perilous journey homeward. what delight we would take in getting up wanton panics in some dusky part of the wood; scampering like frightened deer; pausing to take breath; renewing the panic, and scampering off again, wild with fictitious terror!

Our greatest trial was to pass a dark, lonely pool, covered with pond-lilies, peopled with bull-frogs and water snakes, and haunted by two white cranes. Oh! the terrors of that pond! How our little hearts would beat as we approached it; what fearful glances we would throw around! And if by chance a plash of a wild duck, or the guttural twang of a bull-frog, struck our ears, as we stole quietly by – away we sped, nor paused until completely out of the woods. Then, when I reached home, what a world of adventures and imaginary terrors would I have to relate to my sister Sophy!

As I advanced in years, this turn of mind increased upon me, and became more confirmed. I abandoned myself to the impulses of a romantic imagination, which controlled my studies, and gave a bias to all my habits. My father observed me continually with a book in my hand, and satisfied himself that I was a profound student; but what were my studies? Works of fiction; tales of chivalry; voyages of discovery; travels in the East; everything, in short, that partook of adventure and romance. I well remember with what zest I entered upon that part of my studies which treated of the heathen mythology, and particularly of the sylvan deities. Then indeed my school books became dear to me. The neighbourhood was well calculated to foster the reveries of a mind like mine. It abounded with solitary retreats, wild streams, solemn forests, and silent valleys. I would ramble about for a whole day with a volume of Ovid's *Metamorphoses* in my pocket, and work myself into a kind of self-delusion, so as to identify the surrounding scenes with those of which I had just been reading. I would loiter about a brook that glided through the shadowy depths of the forest, picturing it to myself the haunt of Naiads. I would steal round some bushy copse that opened upon a glade, as if I expected to come suddenly upon Diana and her nymphs, or to behold Pan and his satyrs bounding, with whoop and halloo, through the woodland. I would throw myself, during the panting heats of a summer noon, under the shade of some wide-spreading tree, and muse and dream away the hours, in a state of mental intoxication. I drank in the very light of day, as nectar, and my soul seemed to bathe with ecstasy in the deep blue of a summer sky.

In these wanderings, nothing occurred to jar my feelings, or bring me back to the realities of life. There is a repose in our mighty forests that gives full scope to the imagination. Now and then I would hear the distant sound of the wood-cutter's axe, or the crash of some tree which he had laid low; but these noises, echoing along the quiet landscape, could easily be wrought by fancy into harmony with its illusions. In general, how-ever, the woody recesses of the neighbourhood were peculiarly wild and unfrequented. I could ramble for a whole day, without coming upon any traces of cultivation. The partridge of the wood scarcely seemed to shun my path, and the squirrel, from his nut-tree, would gaze at me for an instant,

with sparkling eye, as if wondering at the un-
wonted intrusion.

I cannot help dwelling on this delicious period of
my life; when as yet I had known no sorrow, nor
experienced any worldly care. I have since studied
much, both of books and men, and of course have
grown too wise to be so easily pleased; yet with
all my wisdom, I must confess I look back with a
secret feeling of regret to the days of happy ignorance, before I had begun to be a philosopher.

It must be evident that I was in a hopeful training
for one who was to descend into the arena of life,
and wrestle with the world. The tutor, also, who
superintended my studies in the more advanced
stage of my education was just fitted to complete
the *fata morgana* which was forming in my mind.
His name was Glencoe. He was a pale,
melancholy-looking man, about forty years of age;
a native of Scotland, liberally educated, and who
had devoted himself to the instruction of youth
from taste rather than necessity; for, as he said, he
loved the human heart, and delighted to study it
in its earlier impulses. My two elder sisters, having
returned home from a city boarding-school, were
likewise placed under his care, to direct their
reading in history and belles-lettres.

We all soon became attached to Glencoe. It is
true, we were at first somewhat prepossessed
against him. His meagre, pallid countenance, his
broad pronunciation, his inattention to the little

forms of society, and an awkward and embarrassed manner, on first acquaintance, were much against him; but we soon discovered that under this unpromising exterior existed the kindest urbanity of temper; the warmest sympathies; the most enthusiastic benevolence. His mind was ingenious and acute. His reading had been various, but more abstruse than profound; his memory was stored, on all subjects, with facts, theories, and quotations, and crowded with crude materials for thinking. These, in a moment of excitement, would be, as it were, melted down, and poured forth in the lava of a heated imagination. At such moments, the change in the whole man was wonderful. His meagre form would acquire a dignity and grace; his long, pale visage would flash with a hectic glow; his eyes would beam with intense speculation; and there would be pathetic tones and deep modulations in his voice, that delighted the ear, and spoke movingly to the heart.

But what most endeared him to us was the kindness and sympathy with which he entered into all our interests and wishes. Instead of curbing and checking our young imaginations with the reins of sober reason, he was a little too apt to catch the impulse and be hurried away with us. He could not withstand the excitement of any sally of feeling or fancy, and was prone to lend heightening tints to the illusive colouring of youthful anticipations.

Under his guidance my sisters and myself soon

entered upon a more extended range of studies; but while they wandered, with delighted minds, through the wide field of history and belles-lettres, a nobler walk was opened to my superior intellect.

The mind of Glencoe presented a singular mixture of philosophy and poetry. He was fond of metaphysics and prone to indulge in abstract speculations, though his metaphysics were somewhat fine spun and fanciful, and his speculations were apt to partake of what my father most irreverently termed 'humbug'. For my part, I delighted in them, and the more especially because they set my father to sleep and completely confounded my sisters. I entered with my accustomed eagerness into this new branch of study. Metaphysics were now my passion. My sisters attempted to accompany me, but they soon faltered, and gave out before they had got halfway through Smith's *Theory of the Moral Sentiments*. I, however, went on, exulting in my strength. Glencoe supplied me with books, and I devoured them with appetite, if not digestion. We walked and talked together under the trees before the house, or sat apart, like Milton's angels, and held high converse upon themes beyond the grasp of ordinary intellects. Glencoe possessed a kind of philosophic chivalry, in imitation of the old peripatetic sages, and was continually dreaming of romantic enterprises in morals, and splendid systems for the improvement of society. He had a fanciful mode of illustrating abstract subjects, peculiarly to my taste; clothing them with the language of poetry, and throwing round them almost the magic hues of fiction. 'How charming,' thought I, 'is divine philosophy'; not harsh and crabbed, as dull fools suppose,

> But a perpetual feast of nectar'd sweets,
> Where no crude surfeit reigns.

I felt a wonderful self-complacency at being on such excellent terms with a man whom I considered on a parallel with sages of antiquity, and looked down with a sentiment of pity on the feebler intellects of my sisters, who could comprehend nothing of metaphysics. It is true, when I attempted to study them by myself, I was apt to get in a fog; but when Glencoe came to my aid, everything was soon as clear to me as day. My ear drank in the beauty of his words; my imagination was dazzled with the splendour of his illustrations. It caught up the sparkling sands of poetry that glittered through his speculations, and mistook them for the golden ore of wisdom. Struck with the facility with which I seemed to imbibe and relish the most abstract doctrines, I conceived a still higher opinion of my mental powers, and was convinced that I also was a philosopher.

I was now verging toward man's estate, and though my education had been extremely irregular – following the caprices of my humour, which I mistook for the impulses of my genius – yet I was regarded with wonder and delight by my mother and sisters, who considered me almost as wise and infallible as I consider myself. This high opinion of me was strengthened by a declamatory habit, which made me an oracle and orator at the domestic board. The time was now at hand, however, that was to put my philosophy to the test.

We had passed through a long winter, and the spring at length opened upon us with unusual sweetness. The soft serenity of the weather; the beauty of the surrounding country; the joyous notes of the birds; the balmy breath of flower and blossom, all combined to fill my bosom with indistinct sensations, and nameless wishes. Amid the soft seductions of the season, I lapsed into a state of utter indolence, both of body and mind.

Philosophy had lost its charms for me. Metaphysics — faugh! I tried to study; took down volume after volume, ran my eye vacantly over a few pages, and threw them by with distaste. I loitered about the house, with my hands in my pockets, and an air of complete vacancy. Something was necessary to make me happy; but what was that something? I sauntered to the apartments of my sisters, hoping their conversation might amuse me. They had walked out, and the room was vacant. On the table lay a volume which they had been reading. It was a novel. I had never read a novel, having conceived a contempt for works of the kind, from hearing them universally condemned. It is true, I had remarked they were universally read; but I considered them beneath the attention of a philosopher, and never would venture to read them, lest I should lessen my mental superiority in the eyes of my sisters. Nay, I had taken up a work of the kind now and then, when I knew my sisters were observing me, looked into it for a moment, and then laid it down, with a slight supercilious smile. On the present occasion, out of mere listlessness, I took up the volume and turned over a few of the first pages. I thought I heard someone coming, and laid it down. I was mistaken; no one was near, and what I had read tempted my curiosity to read a little further. I leaned against a window-frame, and in a few minutes was completely lost in the story. How long I stood there reading I know not, but I believe for nearly two hours. Suddenly I heard my sisters on the stairs, when I thrust the book into my bosom, and the two other volumes which lay near into my pockets, and hurried out of the house to my beloved woods. Here I remained all day beneath the trees, bewildered, bewitched, devouring the contents of these delicious volumes, and only returned to the house when it was too dark to peruse their pages.

This novel finished, I replaced it in my sisters' apartment, and looked for others. Their stock was ample, for they had brought home all that were current in the city; but my appetite demanded an immense supply. All this course of reading was carried on clandestinely, for I was a little ashamed of it, and fearful that my wisdom might be called in question; but this very privacy gave it additional zest. It was 'bread eaten in secret'; it had the charm of a private amour.

But think what must have been the effect of such a course of reading on a youth of my temperament and turn of mind; indulged, too, amid romantic scenery and in the romantic season of the year. It seemed as if I had entered upon a new scene of existence. A train of combustible feelings were lighted up in me, and my soul was all tenderness and passion. Never was youth more completely love-sick, though as yet it was a mere general sentiment, and wanted a definite object. Unfortunately, our neighbourhood was particularly deficient in female society, and I languished in vain for some divinity to whom I might offer up this most uneasy burden of affections. I was at one time seriously enamoured of a lady whom I saw occasionally in my rides, reading at the window of a country-seat; and actually serenaded her with my flute; when, to my confusion, I discovered that she was old enough to be my mother. It was a sad damper to my romance; especially as my father heard of it, and made it the subject of one of those household jokes which he was apt to serve up at every meal-time.

I soon recovered from this check, however, but it was only to relapse into a state of amorous excitement. I passed whole days in the fields, and along the brooks; for there is something in the tender passion that makes us alive to the beauties of nature. A soft sunshiny morning infused a sort of rapture into my breast. The song of the birds melted me to tenderness. I would lie by the side of some rivulet for hours, and form garlands of the flowers on its banks, and muse on ideal beauties, and sigh from the crowd of undefined emotions that swelled my bosom.

In this state of amorous delirium, I was strolling one morning along a beautiful wild brook, which I had discovered in a glen. There was one place where a small waterfall, leaping from among rocks into a natural basin, made a scene such as a poet might have chosen as the haunt of some shy Naiad. It was here I usually retired to banquet on my novels. In visiting the place this morning I traced distinctly, on the margin of the basin, which was of fine clear sand, the prints of a female foot of the most slender and delicate proportions. This was sufficient for an imagination like mine. Robinson Crusoe himself, when he discovered the print of a savage foot on the beach of his lonely island, could not have been more suddenly assailed with thick-coming fancies.

I endeavoured to track the steps, but they only passed for a few paces along the fine sand, and then were lost among the herbage. I remained gazing in reverie upon this passing trace of loveliness. It evidently was not made by any of my sisters, for they knew nothing of this haunt; beside, the foot was smaller than theirs; it was remarkable for its beautiful delicacy.

My eye accidentally caught two or three half-withered wild flowers lying on the ground. The unknown nymph had doubtless dropped them from her bosom! Here was a new document of taste and sentiment. I treasured them up as invaluable relics. The place, too, where I found them, was remarkably picturesque, and the most beautiful part of the brook. It was overhung with a fine elm, entwined with grapevines. She who could select such a spot, who could delight in wild brooks, and wild flowers, and silent solitudes, must have fancy, and feeling, and tenderness; and with all these qualities, she must be beautiful!

But who could be this Unknown that had thus passed by, as in a morning dream, leaving merely flowers and fairy footsteps to tell of her loveliness? There was a mystery in it that bewildered me. It was so vague and disembodied, like those 'airy tongues that syllable men's names' in solitude. Every attempt to solve the mystery was vain. I could hear of no being in the neighbourhood to whom this trace could be ascribed. I haunted the spot, and became daily more and more enamoured. Never, surely, was passion more pure and spiritual, and never lover in more dubious situation. My case could be compared only to that of the amorous prince in the fairy tale of Cinderella; but he had a glass slipper on which to lavish his tenderness. I, alas! was in love with a footstep!

The imagination is alternately a cheat and a dupe;

nay, more, it is the most subtle of cheats, for it cheats itself and becomes the dupe of its own delusions. It conjures up 'airy nothings', gives to them a 'local habitation and a name', and then bows to their control as implicitly as though they were realities. Such was now my case. The good Numa could not more thoroughly have persuaded himself that the nymph Egeria hovered about her sacred fountain and communed with him in spirit, than I had deceived myself into a kind of visionary intercourse with the airy phantom fabricated in my brain. I constructed a rustic seat at the foot of the tree where I had discovered the footsteps. I made a kind of bower there, where I used to pass my mornings reading poetry and romances. I carved hearts and darts on the tree, and hung it with garlands. My heart was full to overflowing, and wanted some faithful bosom into which it might relieve itself. What is a lover without a confidante? I thought at once of my sister Sophy, my early playmate, the sister of my affections. She was so reasonable, too, and of such correct feelings always listening to my words as oracular sayings, and admiring my scraps of poetry as the very inspirations of the muse. From such a devoted, such a rational being, what secrets could I have?

I accordingly took her one morning to my favourite retreat. She looked around, with delighted surprise, upon the rustic seat, the bower, the tree carved with emblems of the tender passion. She turned her eyes upon me to inquire the meaning.

'Oh, Sophy,' exclaimed I, clasping both her hands in mine, and looking earnestly in her face, 'I am in love.'

She started with surprise.

'Sit down,' said I, 'and I will tell you all.'

She seated herself upon the rustic bench, and I went into a full history of the footstep, with all the associations of idea that had been conjured up by my imagination.

Sophy was enchanted; it was like a fairy tale; she had read of such mysterious visitations in books, and the loves thus conceived were always for beings of superior order, and were always happy. She caught the illusion in all its force; her cheek glowed; her eye brightened.

'I dare say she's pretty,' said Sophy.

'Pretty!' echoed I, 'she is beautiful!' I went through all the reasoning by which I had logically proved the fact to my own satisfaction. I dwelt upon the evidences of her taste, her sensibility to the beauties of nature; her soft meditative habit, that delighted in solitude. 'Oh,' said I, clasping my hands, 'to have such a companion to wander through these scenes; to sit with her by this murmuring stream; to wreathe garlands round her brows; to hear the music of her voice mingling with the whisperings of these groves; –'

'Delightful! delightful!' cried Sophy; 'what a sweet creature she must be! She is just the friend I want. How I shall dote upon her! Oh, my dear brother! you must not keep her all to yourself. You must let *me* have some share of her!'

I caught her to my bosom: 'You shall – you shall!' cried I, 'my dear Sophy we will all live for each other!'

The conversation with Sophy heightened the illusions of my mind; and the manner in which she had treated my day-dream identified it with facts and persons and gave it still more the stamp of reality. I walked about as one in a trance, heedless of the world around, and lapped in an elysium of the fancy.

In this mood I met one morning with Glencoe. He accosted me with his usual smile, and was proceeding with some general observations, but paused and fixed on me an inquiring eye.

'What is the matter with you?' said he, 'you seem agitated; has anything in particular happened?'

'Nothing,' said I, hesitating; 'at least nothing worth communicating to you.'

'Nay, my, dear young friend,' said he, 'whatever is of sufficient importance to agitate you is worthy of being communicated to me.'

'Well; but my thoughts are running on what you would think, a frivolous subject.'

'No subject is frivolous that has the power to awaken strong feelings.'

'What think you,' said I, hesitating, 'what think you of love?'

Glencoe almost started at the question. 'Do you call that a frivolous subject?' replied he. 'Believe me, there is none fraught with such deep, such vital interest. If you talk, indeed, of the capricious inclination awakened by the mere charm of perishable beauty, I grant it to be idle in the extreme; but that love which springs from the concordant sympathies of virtuous hearts; that love which is awakened by the perception of moral excellence, and fed by meditation on intellectual as well as personal beauty; that is a passion which refines and ennobles the human heart. Oh, where is there a sight more nearly approaching to the intercourse of angels, than that of two young beings, free from the sins and follies of the world, mingling pure thoughts, and looks, and feelings, and becoming as it were soul of one soul and heart of one heart! How, exquisite the silent converse that they hold; the soft devotion of the eye, that needs no words to make it eloquent! Yes, my friend, if there be anything in this weary world worthy of heaven, it is the pure bliss of such a mutual affection!'

The words of my worthy tutor overcame all further reserve. 'Mr Glencoe,' cried I, blushing still deeper, 'I am in love.'

'And is that what you were ashamed to tell me? Oh, never seek to conceal from your friend so important a secret. If your passion be unworthy, it is for the steady hand of friendship to pluck it forth; if honourable, none but an enemy would seek to stifle it. On nothing does the character and happiness so much depend as on the first affection of the heart. Were you caught by some fleeting and superficial charm – a bright eye, a blooming cheek, a soft voice, or a voluptuous form – I would warn you to beware; I would tell you that beauty is but a passing gleam of the morning, a perishable flower; that accident may becloud and blight it, and that at best it must soon pass away. But were you in love with such a one as I could describe; young in years, but still younger in feelings; lovely in person, but as a type of the mind's beauty; soft in voice, in token of gentleness of spirit; blooming in countenance, like the rosy tints of morning kindling with the promise of a genial day; an eye beaming with the benignity of a happy heart; a cheerful temper, alive to all kind of impulses, and frankly diffusing its own felicity; a self-poised mind, that needs not lean on others for support; an elegant taste, that can embellish solitude, and furnish out its own enjoyments –'

'My dear sir,' cried I, for I could contain myself no longer, 'you have described the very person!'

'Why, then, my dear young friend,' said he, affectionately pressing my hand, 'in God's name, love on!'

For the remainder of the day I was in some such state of dreamy beatitude as a Turk is said to enjoy when under the influence of opium. It must be already manifest how prone I was to bewilder myself with picturings of the fancy, so as to confound them with existing realities. In the present instance, Sophy and Glencoe had contributed to promote the transient delusion. Sophy, dear girl, had as usual joined with me in my castle-building, and indulged in the same train of imaginings, while Glencoe, duped by my enthusiasm, firmly believed that I spoke of a being I had seen and known. By their sympathy with my feelings they in a manner became associated with the Unknown in my mind, and thus linked her with the circle of my intimacy.

In the evening, our family party was assembled in the hall, to enjoy the refreshing breeze. Sophy was playing some favourite Scotch airs on the piano, while Glencoe, seated apart, with his forehead resting on his hand, was buried in one of those pensive reveries that made him so interesting to me.

'What a fortunate being I am!' thought I, 'blessed with such a sister and such a friend! I have only to find out this amiable Unknown, to wed her, and be happy! What a paradise will be my home, graced with a partner of such exquisite refinement! It will be a perfect fairy bower, buried among sweets and roses. Sophy shall live with us, and be the companion of all our enjoyments. Glencoe, too, shall no more be the solitary being that he now appears. He shall have a home with us. He shall have his study, where, when he pleases, he may shut himself up from the world, and bury himself in his own reflections. His retreat shall be sacred; no one shall intrude there; no one but myself, who will visit him now and then, in his seclusion, where we will devise grand schemes together for the improvement of mankind. How delightfully our days will pass, in a round of rational pleasures and elegant employments! Sometimes we will have music; sometimes we will read; sometimes we will wander through the flower garden, when I will smile with complacency on every flower my wife has planted; while in the long winter evenings the ladies will sit at their work, and listen with hushed attention to Glencoe and myself, as we discuss the abstruse doctrines of metaphysics.'

From this delectable reverie, I was startled by my father's slapping me on the shoulder: 'What possesses the lad?' cried he; 'here have I been speaking to you half a dozen times, without receiving an answer.'

'Pardon me, sir,' replied' I; 'I was so completely lost in thought, that I did not hear you.'

'Lost in thought! And pray what were you thinking of? Some of your philosophy, I suppose.'

'Upon my word,' said my sister Charlotte, with an arch laugh, 'I suspect Harry's in love again.'

'And if I were in love, Charlotte,' said I, somewhat nettled, and recollecting Glencoe's enthusiastic eulogy of the passion, 'if I were in love, is that a matter of jest and laughter? Is the tenderest and most fervid affection that can animate the human breast, to be made a matter of cold-hearted ridicule?'

My sister coloured. 'Certainly not, brother! – nor did I mean to make it so, nor to say anything that should wound your feelings. Had I really suspected you had formed some genuine attachment, it would have been sacred in my eyes; but – but,' said she, smiling, as if at some whimsical recollection, 'I thought that you – you might be indulging in another little freak of the imagination.'

'I'll wager any money,' cried my father, 'he has fallen in love again with some old lady at a window!'

'Oh no!' cried my dear sister Sophy, with the most gracious warmth; 'she is young and beautiful.'

'From what I understand,' said Glencoe, rousing himself, 'she must be lovely in mind as in person.'

I found my friends were getting me into a fine scrape. I began to perspire at every pore, and felt my ears tingle.

'Well, but,' cried my father, 'who is she? – what is she? Let us hear something about her.'

This was no time to explain so delicate a matter. I caught up my hat, and vanished out of the house.

The moment I was in the open air, and alone, my heart upbraided me. Was this respectful treatment to my father – to *such* a father, too – who had always regarded me as the pride of his age – the staff of his hopes? It is true, he was apt sometimes to laugh at my enthusiastic flights, and did not treat my philosophy with due respect; but when had he ever thwarted a wish of my heart? Was I then to act with reserve toward him, in a matter which might affect the whole current of my future life? 'I have done wrong,' thought I; 'but it is not too late to remedy it. I will hasten back and open my whole heart to my father!'

I returned accordingly, and was just on the point of entering the house, with my heart full of filial piety, and a contrite speech upon my lips, when I heard a burst of obstreperous laughter from my father, and a loud titter from my two elder sisters.

'A footstep!' shouted he, as soon as he could recover himself, 'in love with a footstep! Why, this beats the old lady at the window!' And then there was another appalling burst of laughter. Had it been a clap of thunder, it could hardly have astounded me more completely. Sophy, in the simplicity of her heart, had told all, and had set my father's risible propensities in full action.

Never was poor mortal so thoroughly crestfallen as myself. The whole delusion was at an end. I drew off silently from the house, shrinking smaller and smaller at every fresh peal of laughter; and wandering about until the family had retired, stole quietly to my bed. Scarce any sleep, however, visited my eyes that night! I lay overwhelmed with mortification, and meditating how I might meet the family in the morning. The idea of ridicule was always intolerable to me; but to endure it on a subject by which my feelings had been so much excited, seemed worse than death. I almost determined, at one time, to get up, saddle my horse, and ride off, I knew not whither.

At length I came to a resolution. Before going down to breakfast, I sent for Sophy, and employed her as ambassador to treat formally in the matter. I insisted that the subject should be buried in oblivion; otherwise I would not show my face at table. It was readily agreed to; for not one of the family would have given me pain for the world. They faithfully kept their promise. Not a word was said of the matter; but there were wry faces, and suppressed titters, that went to my soul; and whenever my father looked me in the face, it was with such a tragic-comical leer – such an attempt to pull down a serious brow upon a whimsical mouth – that I had a thousand times rather he had laughed outright.

For a day or two after the mortifying occurrence just related, I kept as much as possible out of the way of the family, and wandered about the fields and woods by myself. I was sadly out of tune; my feelings were all jarred and unstrung. The birds sang from every grove, but I took no pleasure in their melody; and the flowers of the field bloomed unheeded around me. To be crossed in love is bad enough; but then one can fly to poetry for relief, and turn one's woes to account in soul-subduing stanzas. But to have one's whole passion, object and all, annihilated, dispelled, proved to be such stuff as dreams are made of – or, worse than all, to be turned into a proverb and a jest – what consolation is there in such a case?

I avoided the fatal brook where I had seen the footstep. My favourite resort was now the banks of the Hudson, where I sat upon the rocks and mused upon the current that dimpled by, or the waves that laved the shore; or watched the bright mutations of the clouds, and the shifting lights and shadows of the distant mountain. By degrees a returning serenity stole over my feelings; and a sigh now and then, gentle and easy, and unattended by pain, showed that my heart was recovering its susceptibility.

As I was sitting in this musing mood my eye became gradually fixed upon an object that was borne along by the tide. It proved to be a little pinnace, beautifully modelled, and gaily painted and decorated. It was an unusual sight in this neighbourhood, which was rather lonely; indeed, it was rare to see any pleasure-barks in this part of the river. As it drew nearer, I perceived that there was no one on board; it had apparently drifted from its anchorage. There was not a breath of air; the little bark came floating along on the glassy stream, wheeling about with the eddies. At length it ran aground, almost at the foot of the rock on which I was seated. I descended to the margin of the river, and drawing the bark to shore, admired its light and elegant proportions and the taste with which it was fitted up. The benches were covered with cushions, and its long streamer was of silk. On one of the cushions lay a lady's glove, of delicate size and shape, with beautifully tapered fingers. I instantly seized it and thrust it in my bosom; it seemed a match for the fairy footstep that had so fascinated me.

In a moment all the romance of my bosom was again in a glow. Here was one of the very incidents of fairy tale; a bark sent by some invisible power, some good genius, or benevolent fairy, to waft me to some delectable adventure. I recollected something of an enchanted bark, drawn by white swans, that conveyed a knight down the current of the Rhine, on some enterprise connected with love and beauty. The glove, too, showed that there was a lady fair concerned in the present adventure. It might be a gauntlet of defiance, to dare me to the enterprise.

In the spirit of romance and the whim of the moment, I sprang on board, hoisted the light sail, and pushed from shore. As if breathed by some presiding power, a light breeze at that moment sprang up, swelled out the sail, and dallied with the silken streamer. For a time I glided along under steep umbrageous banks, or across deep sequestered bays; and then stood out over a wide expansion of the river toward a high rocky promontory. It was a lovely evening; the sun was setting in a congregation of clouds that threw the whole heavens in a glow, and were reflected in the river. I delighted myself with all kinds of fantastic fancies, as to what enchanted island, or mystic bower, or, necromantic palace, I was to be conveyed by the fairy bark.

In the revel of my fancy I had not noticed that the gorgeous congregation of clouds which had so much delighted me was in fact a gathering thunder-gust. I perceived the truth too late. The clouds came hurrying on, darkening as they advanced. The whole face of nature was suddenly changed, and assumed that baleful and livid tint predictive of a storm. I tried to gain the shore, but before I could reach it a blast of wind struck the water and lashed it at once into foam. The next moment it overtook the boat. Alas! I was nothing of a sailor; and my protecting fairy forsook me in the moment of peril. I endeavoured to lower the sail; but in so doing I had to quit the helm; the bark was overturned in an instant, and I was thrown into the water. I endeavoured to cling to the wreck, but missed my hold; being a poor swimmer, I soon found myself sinking, but grasped a light oar that was floating by me. It was not sufficient for my support; I again sank beneath the surface; there was a rushing and bubbling sound in my ears, and all sense forsook me.

How long I remained insensible, I know not. I

had a confused notion of being moved and tossed about, and of hearing strange beings and strange voices around me; but all was like a hideous dream. When I at length recovered full consciousness and perception, I found myself in bed in a spacious chamber, furnished with more taste than I had been accustomed to. The bright rays of a morning sun were intercepted by curtains of a delicate rose colour, that gave a soft, voluptuous tinge to every object. Not far from my bed, on a classic tripod, was a basket of beautiful exotic flowers, breathing the sweetest fragrance.

'Where am I? How came I here?'

I tasked my mind to catch at some previous event, from which I might trace up the thread of existence to the present moment. By degrees I called to mind the fairy pinnace, my daring embarkation, my adventurous voyage, and my disastrous shipwreck. Beyond that, all was chaos. How came I here? What unknown region had I landed upon? The people that inhabited it must be gentle and amiable, and of elegant tastes, for they loved downy beds, fragrant flowers, and rose-coloured curtains.

While I lay thus musing, the tones of a harp reached my ear. Presently they were accompanied by a female voice. It came from the room below; but in the profound stillness of my chamber not a modulation was lost. My sisters were all considered good musicians, and sang very tolerably; but I had never heard a voice like this. There was no attempt at difficult execution, or striking effect; but there were exquisite inflections, and tender turns, which art could not reach. Nothing but feeling and sentiment could produce them. It was soul breathed forth in sound. I was always alive to the influence of music; indeed, I was susceptible of voluptuous influences of every kind – sounds, colours, shapes, and fragrant odours. I was the very slave of sensation.

I lay mute and breathless, and drank in every note of this siren strain. It thrilled through my whole frame, and filled my soul with melody and love. I pictured to myself, with curious logic, the form of the unseen musician. Such melodious sounds and exquisite inflections could only be produced by organs of the most delicate flexibility. Such organs do not belong to coarse, vulgar forms; they are the harmonious results of fair proportions and admirable symmetry. A being so organized must be lovely.

Again my busy imagination was at work. I called to mind the Arabian story of a prince, borne away during sleep by a good genius, to the distant abode of a princess of ravishing beauty. I do not pretend to say that I believed in having experienced a similar transportation; but it was my inveterate habit to cheat myself with fancies of the kind, and to give the tinge of illusion to surrounding realities.

The witching sound had ceased, but its vibrations still played round my heart, and filled it with a tumult of soft emotions. At this moment, a self-upbraiding pang shot through my bosom. 'Ah, recreant!' a voice seemed to exclaim, 'is this the stability of thine affections? What! hast thou so soon forgotten the nymph of the fountain? Has one song, idly piped in thine ear, been sufficient to charm away the cherished tenderness of a whole summer?'

The wise may smile – but I am in a confiding mood, and must confess my weakness. I felt a degree of compunction at this sudden infidelity, yet I could not resist the power of present fascination. My peace of mind was destroyed by conflicting claims. The nymph of the fountain came over my memory, with all the associations of fairy footsteps, shady groves, soft echoes, and wild streamlets; but this new passion was produced by a strain of soul-subduing melody, still lingering in my ear, aided by a downy bed, fragrant flowers, and rose-coloured curtains. 'Unhappy youth!' sighed I to myself, 'distracted by such rival passions, and the empire of thy heart thus violently contested by the sound of a voice, and the print of a, footstep!'

I had not remained long in this mood, when I heard the door of the room gently opened. I turned my head to see what inhabitant of this enchanted palace should appear; whether page in green, hideous dwarf, or haggard fairy. It was my own man Scipio. He advanced with cautious step, and was delighted, as he said, to find me so much myself again. My first questions were as to where I was and how I came there? Scipio told me a long story of his having been fishing in a canoe at the time of my hare-brained cruise; of his noticing the gathering squall, and my impending danger; of his hastening to join me, but arriving just in time to snatch me from a watery grave; of the great difficulty in restoring me to animation; and of my being subsequently conveyed, in a state of insensibility, to this mansion.

'But where am I?' was the reiterated demand.

'In the house of Mr Somerville.'

'Somerville – Somerville!' I recollected to have heard that a gentleman of that name had recently taken up his residence at some distance from my father's abode, on the opposite side of the Hudson. He was commonly known by the name of 'French Somerville', from having passed part of his early life in France, and from his exhibiting traces of French taste in his mode of living, and the arrangements of his house. In fact, it was in his pleasure-boat, which had got adrift, that I had made my fanciful and disastrous cruise. All this was simple, straightforward matter of fact, and threatened to demolish all the cobweb romance I had been spinning, when fortunately I again heard the tinkling of a harp. I raised myself in bed, and listened.

'Scipio,' said I, with some little hesitation, 'I heard someone singing just now. Who was it?'

'Oh, that was Miss Julia.'

'Julia! Julia! Delightful! what a name! And, Scipio – is she – is she pretty?'

Scipio grinned from ear to ear. 'Except Miss Sophy, she was the most beautiful young lady he had ever seen.'

I should observe, that my sister Sophia was considered by all the servants a paragon of perfection.

Scipio now offered to remove the basket of flowers; he was afraid their odour might be too powerful; but Miss Julia had given them that morning to be placed in my room.

These flowers, then, had been gathered by the fairy fingers of my unseen beauty; that sweet breath which had filled my ear with melody had passed over them. I made Scipio hand them to me, culled several of the most delicate, and laid them on my bosom.

Mr Somerville paid me a visit not long afterward. He was an interesting study for me, for he was the father of my unseen beauty, and probably resembled her. I scanned him closely. He was a tall and elegant man, with an open, affable manner, and an erect and graceful carriage. His eyes were bluish-grey, and though not dark, yet at times were sparkling and expressive. His hair was dressed and powdered, and being lightly combed up from his forehead, added to the loftiness of his aspect. He was fluent in discourse, but his conversation had the quiet tone of polished society, without any of those bold flights of thought, and picturings of fancy, which I so much admired.

My imagination was a little puzzled, at first, to make out of this assemblage of personal and mental qualities, a picture that should harmonize with my previous idea of the fair unseen. By dint, however, of selecting what it liked, and giving a touch here and a touch there, it soon finished out a satisfactory portrait.

'Julia must be tall,' thought I, 'and of exquisite grace and dignity. She is not quite so courtly as her father, for she has been brought up in the retirement of the country. Neither is she of such vivacious deportment; for the tones of her voice are soft, and plaintive, and she loves pathetic music. She is rather pensive – yet not too pensive; just what is called interesting. Her eyes are like her father's except that they are of a purer blue, and more tender and languishing. She has light hair – not exactly flaxen, for I do not like flaxen hair, but between that and auburn. In a word, she is a tall, elegant, imposing, languishing, blue-eyed, romantic-looking beauty.' And having thus finished her picture, I felt ten times more in love with her than ever.

I felt so much recovered that I would at once have left my room, but Mr Somerville objected to it. He had sent early word to my family of my safety; and my father arrived in the course of the morning. He was shocked at learning the risk I had run, but rejoiced to find me so much restored, and was warm in his thanks to Mr Somerville for his kindness. The other only required, in return, that I might remain two or three days as his guest, to give time for my recovery, and for our forming a closer acquaintance; a request which my father readily granted. Scipio accordingly accompanied my father home, and returned with a supply of clothes, and with affectionate letters from my mother and sisters.

The next morning, aided by Scipio, I made my toilet with rather more care than usual, and descended the stairs with some trepidation, eager to see the original of the portrait which had been so completely pictured in my imagination.

On entering the parlour, I found it deserted. Like the rest of the house, it was furnished in a foreign style. The curtains were of French silk; there were Grecian couches, marble tables, pier-glasses, and chandeliers. What chiefly attracted my eye, were documents of female taste that I saw around me; a piano, with an ample stock of Italian music; a book of poetry lying on the sofa; a vase of fresh flowers on a table, and a portfolio open with a skilful and half-finished sketch of them. In the window was a canary bird, in a gilt cage, and near by, the harp that had been in Julia's arms. Happy harp! But where was the being that reigned in this little empire of delicacies? – that breathed poetry and song, and dwelt among birds and flowers, and rose-coloured curtains?

Suddenly I heard the hall door fly open, the quick pattering of light steps, a wild, capricious strain of music, and the shrill barking of a dog. A light, frolic nymph of fifteen came tripping into the room, playing on a flageolet, with a little spaniel romping after her. Her gypsy hat had fallen back upon her shoulders; a profusion of glossy brown hair was blown in rich ringlets about her face, which beamed through them with the brightness of smiles and dimples.

At sight of me she, stopped short, in the most beautiful confusion, stammered out a word or two about looking for her father, glided out of the door, and I heard her bounding up the staircase, like a frightened fawn, with the little dog barking after her.

When Miss Somerville returned to the parlour, she was quite a different being. She entered, stealing along by her mother's side with noiseless step, and sweet timidity: her hair was prettily adjusted, and a soft blush mantled on her damask cheek. Mr Somerville accompanied the ladies, and introduced me regularly to them. There were many kind enquiries and much sympathy expressed, on the subject of my nautical accident, and some remarks upon the wild scenery of the neighbourhood, with which the ladies seemed perfectly acquainted.

'You must know,' said Mr Somerville, 'that we are great navigators, and delight in exploring every nook and corner of the river. My daughter, too, is

a great hunter of the picturesque, and transfers
every rock and glen to her portfolio. By the way,
my dear, show Mr Mountjoy that pretty scene
you have lately sketched.' Julia complied, blushing, and drew from her portfolio a coloured sketch.
I almost started at the sight. It was my favourite
brook. A sudden thought darted across my mind.
I glanced down my eye, and beheld the divinest
little foot in the world. Oh, blissful conviction!
The struggle of my affections was at an end. The
voice and the footstep were no longer at variance.
Julia Somerville was the nymph of the fountain!

What conversation passed during breakfast I do
not recollect, and hardly was conscious of at the
time, for my thoughts were in complete confusion.
I wished to gaze on Miss Somerville, but did not
dare. Once, indeed, I ventured a glance. She was
at that moment darting a similar one from under a
covert of ringlets. Our eyes seemed shocked by
the rencontre, and fell; hers through the natural
modesty of her sex, mine through a bashfulness
produced by the previous workings of my imagination. That glance, however, went like a sunbeam
to my heart.

A convenient mirror favoured my diffidence,
and gave me the reflection of Miss Somerville's
form. It is true it only presented the back of her
head, but she had the merit of an ancient statue;
contemplate her from any point of view, she was
beautiful. And yet she was totally different from

everything I had before conceived of beauty. She was not the serene, meditative maid that I had pictured the nymph of the fountain; nor the tall, soft, languishing, blue-eyed, dignified being that I had fancied the minstrel of the harp. There was nothing of dignity about her: she was girlish in her appearance, and scarcely of the middle size; but then there was the tenderness of budding youth; the sweetness of the half-blown rose, when not a tint or perfume has been withered or exhaled; there were smiles and dimples, and all the soft witcheries of ever-varying expression. I wondered that I could ever have admired any other style of beauty.

After breakfast, Mr Somerville departed to attend to the concerns of his estate, and gave me in charge of the ladies. Mrs Somerville also was called away by household cares, and I was left alone with Julia! Here, then, was the situation which of all others I had most coveted. I was in the presence of the lovely being that had so long been the desire of my heart. We were alone; propitious opportunity for a lover! Did I seize upon it? Did I break out in one of my accustomed rhapsodies? No such thing! Never was being more awkwardly embarrassed.

'What can be the cause of this?' thought I. 'Surely, I cannot stand in awe of this young girl. I am of course her superior in intellect, and am never embarrassed in company with my tutor, notwithstanding all his wisdom.'

It was passing strange. I felt that if she were an old woman, I should be quite at my ease; if she were even an ugly woman, I should make out very well: it was her beauty that overpowered me. How little do lovely women know what awful beings they are, in the eyes of inexperienced youth! Young men brought up in the fashionable circles of our cities will smile at all this. Accustomed to mingle incessantly in female society, and to have the romance of the heart deadened by a thousand frivolous flirtations, women are nothing but women in their eyes; but to a susceptible youth like myself, brought up in the country, they are perfect divinities.

Miss Somerville was at first a little embarrassed herself; but, somehow or other, women have a natural adroitness in recovering their self-possession; they are more alert in their minds, and graceful in their manners. Beside, I was but an ordinary personage in Miss Somerville's eyes; she was not under the influence of such a singular course of imaginings as had surrounded her, in my eyes, with the illusions of romance. Perhaps, too, she saw the confusion in the opposite camp and gained courage from the discovery. At any rate she was the first to take the field.

Her conversation, however, was only on commonplace topics, and in an easy, well-bred style. I endeavoured to respond in the same manner; but I was strangely incompetent to the task. My ideas were frozen up; even words seemed to fail me. I was excessively vexed at myself, for I wished to be uncommonly elegant. I tried two or three times to turn a pretty thought, or to utter a fine sentiment; but it would come forth so trite, so forced, so mawkish, that I was ashamed of it. My very voice sounded discordantly, though, I sought to modulate it into the softest tones. 'The truth is,' thought I to myself, 'I cannot bring my mind down to the small talk necessary for young girls; it is too masculine and robust for the mincing measure of parlour gossip. I am a philosopher – and that accounts for it.'

The entrance of Mrs Somerville at length gave me relief. I at once breathed freely, and felt a vast deal of confidence come over me. 'This is strange,' thought I, 'that the appearance of another woman should revive my courage; that I should be a better match for two women than one. However, since it is so, I will take advantage of the circumstance, and let this young lady see that I am not so great a simpleton as she probably thinks me.'

I accordingly took up the book of poetry which lay upon the sofa. It was Milton's *Paradise Lost*. Nothing could have been more fortunate; it afforded a fine scope for my favourite vein of grandiloquence. I went largely into a discussion of its merits, or rather an enthusiastic eulogy of them. My observations were addressed to Mrs Somerville, for I found I could talk to her with more ease than to her daughter. She appeared alive to the beauties of the poet, and disposed to meet me in the discussion; but it was not my object to hear her talk; it was to talk myself. I anticipated all she had to say, overpowered her with the copiousness of my ideas, and supported and illustrated them by long citations from the author.

While thus holding forth, I cast a side glance to see how Miss Somerville was affected. She had some embroidery stretched on a frame before her, but had paused in her labour, and was looking down as if lost in mute attention. I felt a glow of self-satisfaction, but I recollected, at the same time, with a kind of pique, the advantage she had enjoyed over me in our tête-à-tête. I determined to push my triumph, and accordingly kept on with redoubled ardour, until I had fairly exhausted my subject, or rather my thoughts.

I had scarce come to a full stop, when Miss Somerville raised her eyes from the work on which they had been fixed, and turning to her mother, observed: 'I have been considering, mamma, whether to work these flowers plain, or in colours.'

Had an ice-bolt shot to my heart, it could not have chilled me more effectually. 'What a fool,' thought I, 'have I been making myself – squandering away fine thoughts, and fine language, upon a light mind, and an ignorant ear! This girl knows nothing of poetry. She has no soul, I fear, for its beauties. Can any one have real sensibility of heart, and not be alive to poetry! However, she is

young; this part of her education has been ne-
glected: there is time enough to remedy it. I will
be her preceptor. I will kindle in her mind the
sacred flame, and lead her through the fairy land
of song. But after all, it is rather unfortunate that
I should have fallen in love with a woman who
knows nothing of poetry.'

I passed a day not altogether satisfactory. I was a
little disappointed that Miss Somerville did not
show any poetical feeling. 'I am afraid, after all,'
said I to myself, 'she is light and girlish, and more
fitted to pluck wild flowers, play on the flageolet,
and romp with little dogs, than to converse with a
man of my turn.'

I believe, however, to tell the truth, I was more
out of humour with myself. I thought I had made
the worst first appearance that ever hero made,
either in novel or fairy tale. I was out of all
patience, when I called to mind my awkward
attempts at ease and elegance in the tête-à-
tête. And then my intolerable long lecture about
poetry to catch the applause of a heedless auditor!
But there I was not to blame. I had certainly been
eloquent: it was her fault that the eloquence was
wasted. To meditate upon the embroidery of a
flower, when I was expatiating on the beauties of
Milton! She might at least have admired the
poetry, if she did not relish the manner in which
it was delivered: though that was not despicable,
for I had recited passages in my best style, which

my mother and sisters had always considered equal to a play. 'Oh, it is evident,' thought I, 'Miss Somerville has very little soul!'

Such were my fancies and cogitations during the day, the greater part of which was spent in my chamber, for I was still languid. My evening was passed in the drawing-room, where I overlooked Miss Somerville's portfolio of sketches.

They were executed with great taste, and showed a nice observation of the peculiarities of nature. They were all her own, and free from those cunning tints and touches of the drawing-master, by which young ladies' drawings, like their heads, are dressed up for company. There was no garish and vulgar trick of colours, either; all was, executed with singular truth and simplicity.

'And yet,' thought I, 'this little being, who has so pure an eye to take in, as in a limpid brook, all the graceful forms and magic tints of nature, has no soul for poetry!'

Mr Somerville, toward the latter part of the evening, observing my eye to wander occasionally to the harp, interpreted and met my wishes with his accustomed civility.

'Julia, my dear,' said he, 'Mr Mountjoy would like to hear a little music from your harp; let us hear, too, the sound of your voice.'

Julia immediately complied, without any of that hesitation and difficulty, by which young ladies are apt to make company pay dear for bad music.

She sang a sprightly strain, in a brilliant style, that came trilling playfully over the ear; and the bright eye and dimpling smile showed that her little heart danced with the song. Her pet canary bird, who hung close by, was wakened by the music, and burst forth into an emulating strain. Julia smiled with a pretty air of defiance, and played louder.

After some time, the music changed, and ran into a plaintive strain, in a minor key. Then it was, that all the former witchery of her voice came over me; then it was that she seemed tossing from the heart and to the heart. Her fingers moved about the chords as if they scarcely touched them. Her whole manner and appearance changed; her eyes beamed with the softest expression; her countenance, her frame, all seemed subdued into tenderness. She rose from the harp, leaving it still vibrating with sweet sounds, and moved toward her father to bid him good night.

His eyes had been fixed on her intently, during her performance. As she came before him he parted her shining ringlets with both his hands, and looked down with the fondness of a father on her innocent face,. The music seemed still lingering in its lineaments, and the action of her father brought a moist gleam in her eye. He kissed her fair forehead, after the French mode of parental caressing: 'Good night, and God bless you,' said he, 'my good little girl!'

Julia tripped away, with a tear in her eye, a

dimple in her cheek, and a light heart in her bosom. I thought it the prettiest picture of paternal and filial affection I had ever seen.

When I retired to bed, a new train of thoughts crowded into my brain. 'After all,' said I to myself, 'it is clear this girl has a soul, though she was not moved by my eloquence. She has all the outward signs and evidences of poetic feeling. She paints well, and has an eye for nature. She is a fine musician, and enters into the very soul of song. What a pity that she knows nothing of poetry! But we will see what is to be done. I am irretrievably in love with her; what then am I to do? Come down to the level of her mind, or endeavour to raise her to some kind of intellectual equality with myself? That is the most generous course. She will look up to me as a benefactor. I shall become associated in her mind with the lofty thoughts and harmonious graces of poetry. She is apparently docile: beside, the difference of our ages will give me an ascendancy over her. She cannot be over sixteen years of age, and I am full turned of twenty.' So, having built this most delectable of air-castles, I fell asleep.

The next morning I was quite a different being. I no longer felt fearful of stealing a glance at Julia; on the contrary, I contemplated her steadily, with the benignant eye of a benefactor. Shortly after breakfast I found myself alone with her, as I had on the preceding morning; but I felt nothing of the awkwardness of our previous tête-à-tête. I was elevated by the consciousness of my intellectual superiority, and should almost have felt a sentiment of pity for the ignorance of the lovely little being, if I had not felt also the assurance that I should be able to dispel it. 'But it is time,' thought I, 'to open school.'

Julia was occupied in arranging some music on her piano. I looked over two or three songs; they were Moore's Irish melodies.

'These are pretty things!' said I, flirting the leaves over lightly, and giving a slight shrug, by way of qualifying the opinion.

'Oh, I love them of all things,' said Julia, 'they're so touching!'

'Then you like them for the poetry,' said I with an encouraging smile.

'Oh yes'; she thought them charmingly written.

Now was my time. 'Poetry,' said I, assuming a didactic attitude and air, 'poetry is one of the most pleasing studies that can occupy a youthful mind. It renders us susceptible of the gentle impulses of humanity, and cherishes a delicate perception of all that is virtuous and elevated in morals, and graceful and beautiful in physics. It'–

I was going on in a style that would have graced a professor of rhetoric, when I saw a light smile playing about Miss Somerville's mouth, and that she began to turn over the leaves of a music-book. I recollected her inattention to my discourse of the preceding morning. 'There is no fixing her light mind,' thought I, 'by abstract theory; we will proceed practically.' As it happened, the identical volume of Milton's *Paradise Lost* was lying at hand.

'Let me recommend to you, my young friend,' said I, in one of those tones of persuasive admonition, which I had so often loved in Glencoe, 'let me recommend to you this admirable poem; you will find in it sources of intellectual enjoyment far superior to those songs which have delighted you.' Julia looked at the book, and then at me, with a whimsically dubious air. 'Milton's *Paradise Lost?*' said she; 'oh, I know the greater part of that by heart.'

I had not expected to find my pupil so far advanced; however, the *Paradise Lost* is a kind of school-book, and its finest passages are given to young ladies as tasks.

'I find,' said I to myself, 'I must not treat her as so complete a novice; her inattention yesterday could not have proceeded from absolute ignorance, but merely from a want of poetic feeling. I'll try her again'

I now determined to dazzle her with my own erudition, and launched into a harangue that would have done honour to an institute. Pope, Spenser, Chaucer, and the old dramatic writers were all dipped into, with the excursive flight of a swallow. I did not confine myself to English poets, but gave a glance at the French and Italian schools; I passed over Ariosto in full wing, but

paused on Tasso's *Jerusalem Delivered*. I dwelt on
the character of Clorinda: 'There's a character,'
said I, 'that you will find well worthy a woman's
study. It shows to what exalted heights of heroism
the sex can rise, how gloriously they may share
even in the stern concerns of men.'

'For my part,' said Julia, gently taking advantage of a pause, 'for my part, I prefer the character
of Sophronia.'

I was thunderstruck. She then had read Tasso!
This girl that I had been treating as an ignoramus
in poetry! She proceeded with a slight glow of the
cheek, summoned up perhaps by a casual glow of
feeling:

'I do not admire those masculine heroines,' said
she, 'who aim at the bold qualities of the opposite
sex. Now Sophronia only exhibits the real qualities
of a woman, wrought up to their highest excitement. She is modest, gentle, and retiring, as it
becomes a woman to be; but she has all the
strength of affection proper to a woman. She
cannot fight for her people as Clorinda does, but
she can offer herself up, and die to serve them.
You may admire Clorinda, but you surely would
be more apt to love Sophronia; at least,' added
she, suddenly appearing to recollect herself, and
blushing at having launched into such a discussion, 'at least that is what papa observed when we
read the poem together.'

'Indeed,' said I, dryly, for I felt disconcerted
and nettled at being unexpectedly lectured by my

pupil; 'indeed, I do not exactly recollect the passage.'

'Oh,' said Julia, 'I can repeat it to you;' and she immediately gave it in Italian.

Heavens and earth! – here was a situation! I knew no more of Italian than I did of the language of Psalmanazar. What a dilemma for a would-be-wise man to be placed in! I saw Julia waited for my opinion.

'In fact,' said I, hesitating, 'I – I do not exactly understand Italian.'

'Oh,' said Julia, with the utmost naïveté, 'I have no doubt it is very beautiful in the translation.'

I was glad to break up school, and get back to my chamber, full of the mortification which a wise man in love experiences on finding his mistress wiser than himself. 'Translation! translation!' muttered I to myself, as I jerked the door shut behind me: 'I am surprised my father has never had me instructed in the modern languages. They are all important. What is the use of Latin and Greek? No one speaks them; but here, the moment I make my appearance in the world, a little girl slaps Italian in my face. However, thank heaven, a language is easily learned. The moment I return home, I'll set about studying Italian; and to prevent future surprise, I will study Spanish and German at the same time; and 'if any young lady attempts to quote Italian upon me again, I'll bury her under a heap of High Dutch poetry!' I felt now like some mighty chieftain, who has carried the war into a weak country, with full confidence of success, and been repulsed and obliged to draw off his forces from before some inconsiderable fortress.

'However,' thought I, 'I have as yet brought only my light artillery into action; we shall see what is to be done with my heavy ordnance. Julia is evidently well versed in poetry; but it is natural she should be so; it is allied to painting and music, and is congenial to the light graces of the female character. We will try her on graver themes.'

I felt all my pride awakened; it even for a time swelled higher than my love. I was determined completely to establish my mental superiority, and subdue the intellect of this little being; it would then be time to sway the sceptre of gentle empire, and win the affections of her heart.

Accordingly, at dinner I again took the field, *en potence*. I now addressed myself to Mr Somerville, for I was about to enter upon topics in which a young girl like her could not be well versed. I led, or rather forced, the conversation into a vein of historical erudition, discussing several of the most prominent facts of ancient history, and accompanying them with sound, indisputable apothegms.

Mr Somerville listened to me with, the air of a man receiving information. I was encouraged, and went on gloriously from theme to theme of school declamation. I sat with Marius on the ruins of Carthage; I defended the bridge with Horatius

Cocles; thrust my hand into the flame with Marius Scaevola, and plunged with Curtius into the yawning gulf; I fought side by side with Leonidas, at the straits of Thermopylae and was going full drive into the battle of Plataea, when my memory, which is the worst in the world, failed me, just as I wanted the name of the Lacedaemonian commander.

'Julia, my dear,' said Mr Somerville, 'perhaps you may recollect the name of which Mr Mountjoy is in quest?'

Julia coloured slightly. 'I believe,' said she, in a low voice, 'I believe it was Pausanias.'

This unexpected sally, instead of re-enforcing me, threw my whole scheme of battle into confusion, and the Athenians remained unmolested in the field.

I am half inclined, since, to think Mr Somerville meant this as a sly hit at my schoolboy pedantry; but he was too well bred not to seek to relieve me from my mortification. 'Oh!' said he, 'Julia is our family book of reference for names, dates, and distances, and has an excellent memory for history and geography.'

I now became desperate; as a last resource I turned to metaphysics. 'If she is a philosopher in petticoats,' thought I, 'it is all over with me.' Here, however, I had the field to, myself. I gave chapter and verse of my tutor's lectures, heightened by all his poetical illustrations; I even went further than he had ever ventured, and plunged into such depths of metaphysics, that I was in danger of sticking in the mire at the bottom. Fortunately, I had auditors who apparently could not detect my flounderings. Neither Mr Somerville nor his daughter offered the least interruption.

When the ladies had retired, Mr Somerville sat some time with me; and as I was no longer anxious to astonish, I permitted myself to listen, and found that he was really agreeable. He was quite communicative, and from his conversation I was enabled to form a juster idea of his daughter's character, and the mode in which she had been brought up. Mr Somerville had mingled much with the world, and with what is termed fashionable society. He had experienced its cold elegancies and gay insincerities; its dissipation of the spirits and squanderings of the heart. Like many men of the world, though he had wandered too far from nature ever to return to it, yet he had the good taste and good feeling to look back fondly to its simple delights, and to determine that his child, if possible, should never leave them. He had superintended her education with scrupulous care, storing her mind with the graces of polite literature, and with such knowledge as would enable it to furnish its own amusement and occupation, and giving her all the accomplishments that sweeten and enliven the circle of domestic life. He had been particularly sedulous to exclude all fashionable affectations; all false sentiment, false sensibility, and false romance. 'Whatever advantages she may possess,' said he, 'she is quite unconscious of them. She is a capricious little being, in everything but her affections; she is, however, free from art; simple, ingenuous, amiable, and, I thank God! happy.'

Such was the eulogy of a fond father, delivered with a tenderness that touched me. I could not help making a casual inquiry, whether, among the graces of polite literature, he had included a slight tincture of metaphysics. He smiled, and told me he had not.

On the whole, when, as usual, that night, I summed up the day's observations on my pillow, I was not altogether dissatisfied. 'Miss Somerville,' said I, 'loves poetry, and I like her the better for it. She has the advantage of me in Italian: agreed; what is it to know a variety of languages, but merely to have a variety of sounds to express the same idea? Original thought is the ore of the mind; language is but the accidental stamp and coinage by which it is put into circulation. If I can furnish an original idea, what care I how many languages she can translate it into? She may be able also to quote names, and dates, and latitudes better than I; but that is a mere effort of the memory. I admit she is more accurate in history and geography than I; but then she knows nothing of metaphysics.'

I had now sufficiently recovered to return home; yet I could not think of leaving Mr Somerville's

without having a little further conversation with
him on the subject of his daughter's education.

'This Mr Somerville,' thought I, 'is a very
accomplished, elegant man; he has seen a good
deal of the world, and, upon the whole, has prof-
ited by what he has seen. He is not without
information, and, as far as he thinks, appears to
think correctly; but after all, he is rather superficial, and does not think profoundly. He seems to
take no delight in those metaphysical abstractions
that are the proper aliment of masculine minds.' I
called to mind various occasions in which I had
indulged largely in metaphysical discussions, but
could recollect no instance where I had been able
to draw him out. He had listened, it is true, with
attention, and smiled as if in acquiescence, but
had always appeared to avoid reply. Beside, I had
made several sad blunders in the glow of eloquent
declamation but he had never interrupted me, to
notice and correct them, as he would have done
had he been versed in the theme.

'Now, it is really a great pity,' resumed I, 'that
he should have the entire management of Miss
Somerville's education. What a vast advantage it
would be, if she could be put for a little time
under the superintendence of Glencoe. He would
throw some deeper shades of thought into her
mind, which at present is all sunshine; not but
that Mr Somerville has done very well, as far as
he has gone; but then he has merely prepared the
soil for the strong plants of useful knowledge. She

is well versed in the leading facts of history, and the general course of belles-lettres,' said I; 'a little more philosophy would do wonders.'

I accordingly took occasion to ask Mr Somerville for a few moments' conversation in his study, the morning I was to depart. When we were alone I opened the matter fully to him. I commenced with the warmest eulogium of Glencoe's powers of mind, and vast acquirements, and ascribed to him all my proficiency in the higher branches of knowledge. I begged, therefore, to recommend him as a friend calculated to direct the studies of Miss Somerville; to lead her mind, by degrees, to the contemplation of abstract principles, and to produce habits of philosophical analysis; 'which,' added I, gently smiling, 'are not often cultivated by young ladies.' I ventured to hint, in addition, that he would find Mr Glencoe a most valuable and interesting acquaintance for himself; one who would stimulate and evolve the powers of his mind; and who might open to him tracts of inquiry and speculation, to which perhaps he had hitherto been a stranger.

Mr Somerville listened with grave attention. When I had finished, he thanked me in the politest manner for the interest I took in the welfare of his daughter and himself. He observed that, as regarded himself, he was afraid he was too old to benefit by the instruction of Mr Glencoe, and that as to his daughter, he was afraid her mind was but little fitted for the study of metaphysics. 'I do not wish,' continued he, 'to strain her intellects with subjects they cannot grasp, but to make her familiarly acquainted with those that are within the limits of her capacity. I do not pretend to prescribe the boundaries of female genius, and am far from indulging the vulgar opinion that women are unfitted by nature for the highest intellectual pursuits. I speak only with reference to my daughter's tastes and talents. She will never make a learned woman; nor, in truth, do I desire it; for such is the jealousy of our sex, as to mental as well as physical ascendancy, that a learned woman is not always the happiest. I do not wish my daughter to excite envy, nor to battle with the prejudices of the world; but to glide peaceably through life, on the good will and kind opinion of her friends. She has ample employment for her little head, in the course I have marked out for her; and is busy at present with some branches of natural history, calculated to awaken her perceptions to the beauties and wonders of nature, and to the inexhaustible volume of wisdom constantly spread open before her eyes. I consider that woman most likely to make an agreeable companion, who can draw topics of pleasing remark from every natural object; and most likely to be cheerful and contented, who is continually sensible of the order, the harmony, and the invariable beneficence, that reign throughout the beautiful world we inhabit.

'But,' added he, smiling, 'I am betraying myself into a lecture, instead of merely giving a reply to your kind offer. Permit me to take the liberty, in return, of inquiring a little about your own pursuits. You speak of having finished your education; but of course you have a line of private study and mental occupation marked out; for you must know the importance, both in point of interest and happiness, of keeping the mind employed. May I ask what system you observe in your intellectual exercises?'

'Oh, as to system,' I observed, 'I could never bring myself into any thing of the kind. I thought it best to let my genius take its own course, as it always acted the most vigorously when stimulated by inclination.'

Mr Somerville shook his head. 'This same genius,' said he, 'is a wild quality, that runs away with our most promising young men. It has become so much the fashion, too, to give it the reins, that it is now thought an animal of too noble and generous a nature to be brought to harness. But it is all a mistake. Nature never designed these high endowments to run riot through society, and throw the whole system into confusion. No, my dear sir, genius, unless it acts upon system, is very apt to be a useless quality to society; sometimes an injurious, and certainly a very uncomfortable one, to its possessor. I have had many opportunities of seeing the progress through life of young men who were accounted geniuses, and have found it too often end in early exhaustion and bitter disappointment; and have as often noticed that these effects might be traced to a total want of system. There were no habits of business, of steady purpose, and regular application, superinduced upon the mind; everything was left to chance and impulse, and native luxuriance, and everything of course ran to waste and wild entanglement. Excuse me if I am tedious on this point, for I feel solicitous to impress it upon you, being an error extremely prevalent in our country and one into which too many of our youth have fallen. I am happy, however, to observe the zeal which still appears to actuate you for the acquisition of knowledge, and augur every good from the elevated bent of your ambition. May I ask what has been your course of study for the last six months?'

Never was question more unluckily timed. For the last six months I had been absolutely buried in novels and romances.

Mr Somerville perceived that the question was embarrassing, and with his invariable good breeding, immediately resumed the conversation, without waiting for a reply. He took care, however, to turn it in such a way as to draw from me an account of the whole manner in which I had been educated, and the various currents of reading into which my mind had run. He then went on to discuss, briefly but impressively, the different branches of knowledge, most important to a young man in my situation; and to my surprise I found him a complete master of those studies on which I had supposed him ignorant, and on which I had been descanting so confidently.

He complimented me, however, very graciously, upon the progress I had made, but advised me for the present to turn my attention to the physical rather than the moral sciences. 'These studies,' said he, 'store a man's mind with valuable facts, and at the same time repress self-confidence, by letting him know how boundless are the realms of knowledge, and how little we can possibly know. Whereas metaphysical studies, though of an ingenious order of intellectual employment, are apt to bewilder some minds with vague speculations. They never know how far they have advanced, or what may be the correctness of their favourite theory. They render many of our young men verbose and declamatory, and prone to mistake the aberrations of their fancy for the inspirations of divine philosophy.'

I could not but interrupt him, to assent to the truth of these remarks, and to say that it had been my lot, in the course of my limited experience, to encounter young men of the kind, who had overwhelmed me by their verbosity.

Mr Somerville smiled. 'I trust,' said he, kindly, 'that you will guard against these errors. Avoid the eagerness with which a young man is apt to hurry into conversation, and to utter the crude and ill-digested notions which he has picked up in his recent studies. Be assured that extensive and accurate knowledge is the slow acquisition of a

studious lifetime; that a young man, however preg-
nant his wit, and prompt his talent, can have
mastered but the rudiments of learning, and, in a
manner, attained the implements of study. Whatever may have been your past assiduity, you must
be sensible that as yet you have but reached the
threshold of true knowledge; but at the same time,
you have the advantage that you are still very
young, and have amply time to learn.'

Here our conference ended. I walked out of the
study, a very different being from what I was on
entering it. I had gone in with the air of a professor
about to deliver a lecture; I came out like a student
who had failed in his examination, and been de-
graded in his class.

'Very young,' and 'on the threshold of knowledge'! This was extremely flattering, to one who
had considered himself an accomplished scholar,
and profound philosopher.

'It is singular,' thought I; 'there seems to have
been a spell upon my faculties, ever since I have
been in this house. I certainly have not been able
to do myself justice. Whenever I have undertaken
to advise, I have had the tables turned upon me.
It must be that I am strange and diffident among
people I am not accustomed to. I wish they could
hear me talk at home!'

'After all,' added I, on further reflection, 'after
all, there is a great deal of force in what Mr
Somerville has said. Somehow or other, these
men of the world do now and then hit upon

remarks that would do credit to a philosopher. Some of his general observations came so home, that I almost thought they were meant for myself. His advice about adopting a system of study is very judicious. I will immediately put it in practice. My mind shall operate henceforward with the regularity of clockwork.'

How far I succeeded in adopting this plan, how I fared in the further pursuit of knowledge, and how I succeeded in my suit to Julia Somerville, may afford matter for a further communication to the public, if this simple record of my early life is fortunate enough to excite any curiosity.

AESOP'S FABLES
Translated by S. A. Handford

Many of these tales are so well known they have given us phrases we use every day – like dog in the manger or sour grapes – but even the rarer ones seem familiar, because their simple morals are based on universal truths. From the tortoise and the hare or the boy who cried wolf to the treacherous partridge or the big and little fish, Aesop's wise and foolish creatures are a lasting delight.

ALADDIN AND OTHER TALES FROM THE ARABIAN NIGHTS
Retold by N. J. Dawood

The ragamuffin Aladdin finds an old lamp which makes his fortune; a prince disappears on a flying horse; a falcon proves wiser than a king . . . These tales of kings and princes, magicians, talking beasts, and shrewd working people, daily entertainment in India, Persia and Arabia over a thousand years ago, are retold especially for children in this vivid, straightforward collection.

AROUND THE WORLD IN EIGHTY DAYS
Jules Verne

For a bet, Phileas Fogg sets out with his servant
Passepartout to achieve an incredible journey –
from London to Paris, Brindisi, Suez, Bombay,
Calcutta, Singapore, Hong Kong, San Francisco,
New York and back to London again, all in just
eighty days! There are many alarms and surprises
along the way – and a last-minute setback that
makes all the difference between winning
and losing.

AT THE BACK OF THE NORTH WIND
George MacDonald

One night the North Wind comes into the hayloft
where Diamond sleeps, and takes him flying with
her. It is the start of many adventures for the
coachman's son, with hardships to face and
challenges to master by day, and his strange,
beautiful and sometimes terrible journeys by night,
before at last he reaches the country at the back of
the North Wind.

THE CANTERBURY TALES
Geoffrey Chaucer
Retold by Geraldine McCaughrean

A lively retelling of the famous medieval classic.

One fine spring day, thirty pilgrims set off from Harry Bailey's inn in Southwark for the shrine of Thomas à Becket in Canterbury. The innkeeper makes an offer that none of the travellers can refuse: a free dinner at his inn, on their return, to the person who can tell the best story. So begins the assortment of tales from such varied characters as the Knight, the Wife of Bath, the Miller and many more.

THE CORAL ISLAND
R. M. Ballantyne

Fifteen-year-old Ralph, mischievous young Peterkin and clever, brave Jack are shipwrecked on a coral reef with only a telescope and a broken penknife between them. At first the island seems a paradise, with its plentiful foods and wealth of natural wonders. But then a party of cannibals arrives, and after that a pirate ship . . .

THE ENCHANTED CASTLE
E. Nesbit

Gerald, Cathy and Jimmy wake a beautiful
princess from her hundred year sleep in an
enchanted garden. It's really only Mabel, the
housekeeper's niece – but the garden really is
enchanted, and the ring she slips on really is
magic! The children find themselves in some
funny, some awkward, some frightening and some
absolutely magical situations before everything
gets sorted out.

GREYFRIARS BOBBY
Eleanor Atkinson

Bobby, an active Skye terrier, adores his master
Auld Jock, and when the old man dies, Bobby
refuses to leave his grave in Greyfriars Churchyard
in Edinburgh. By day, he plays with the local
orphans and eats at a nearby tavern, but, in spite of
anything even the Lord Provost himself can do,
every night for fourteen years Bobby returns
faithfully to sleep by his master.

HANS ANDERSEN'S FAIRY TALES
Translated by Naomi Lewis

Chosen and translated by Naomi Lewis, this
selection of Hans Christian Andersen's fairy tales
includes all the favourites as well as some less
familiar stories. Here are 'Thumbelina', 'The
Snow Queen', and 'The Emperor's New Clothes',
and also the delightful 'Dance, Dolly, Dance' and
'The Goblin at the Grocer's', making a perfect
introduction to the 'best-loved, best-known Dane
in all the world

HEIDI
Johanna Spyri

Heidi is five when she is sent to live with her
grandfather in his lonely hut high in the Alps. She
quickly grows to love her carefree new life with
him in the mountain air, and the old man comes to
love her too. They are both unhappy when Heidi is
sent away again, to a family in town, but she soon
manages to get home to her Alps – and to share
her happiness with her new friends.

KIM
Rudyard Kipling

Reared in the teeming streets of India at the turn
of the century, the orphan Kim is the 'Friend of all
the World', an imp with an endless interest in the
extraordinary characters he meets daily. One of
them, an old Tibetan lama, sets him on the path
that will lead him to travel the Great Trunk Road,
pass an unhappy time at St Xavier's School, and
become a spy for the British . . .

LITTLE LORD FAUNTLEROY
Frances Hodgson Burnett

It is quite a shock for a seven-year-old boy to be
whisked away from the New York streets to an
English stately home and be told he is to inherit a
title and a fortune. It is very daunting to have to
face such a crotchety and selfish grandfather. But
then, little Lord Fauntleroy is a very
unusual boy . . .

MYTHS OF THE NORSEMEN
Roger Lancelyn Green

Yggdrasill the World Tree, Odin's wanderings, Thor's hammer, the death of Baldur, Freya the Bride, the vision of Ragnarok – tales told since time immemorial are given fresh vigour in this version, written as a continuous narrative. Peopled with Frost Giants and Valkyries, Norns and all the gods of Asgard, it brings to life the harsh but exciting world of the old Norsemen.

REBECCA OF SUNNYBROOK FARM
Kate Douglas Wiggin

When Rebecca comes from the chaotic family farm to live with her spinster aunts in Riverboro, strict Miranda and gentle Jane don't know how to cope with a wild and zestful ten-year-old – nor she with them. But Rebecca is the most likeable, energetic, enthusiastic girl anyone ever met, and it turns out her mother is right: this chance is just what she needs. And Riverboro is never the same again either!

SINDBAD THE SAILOR AND OTHER TALES FROM THE ARABIAN NIGHTS
Retold by N. J. Dawood

Sindbad, shipwrecked on exotic shores inhabited by mythical beasts and flying men; the amazing adventures of the Barber of Baghdad's six brothers; how Ali Baba outwitted the forty thieves . . . The daily entertainment of everyday people over a thousand years ago, these Arabian, Indian and Persian tales are full of magic and excitement.

TALES OF ANCIENT EGYPT
Roger Lancelyn Green

These stories include the great myths – of Amen-Ra, who created all the creatures in the world; of Isis, searching the waters for her dead husband Osiris; of the Bennu Bird and the Book of Thoth. But there are also tales told for pleasure, about magic, treasure and adventure – even the first ever Cinderella story.

PUFFIN CLASSICS

WHITE FANG
Jack London

In the desolate, frozen wilds of north-west Canada,
a wolf-cub soon finds himself the sole survivor of
the litter. Son of Kiche – half-wolf, half-dog – and
the ageing wolf One Eye, he is thrust into a savage
world where each day becomes a fight to stay alive.

THE WIZARD OF OZ
L. Frank Baum

When a cyclone hits her Kansas home, Dorothy
and her dog Toto are whisked to the magical land
of Oz. To find her way back to Kansas, she must
follow the yellow brick road to the City of
Emeralds where the great Wizard lives. But first
Dorothy, Toto and their companions the Tin
Woodman, Scarecrow and Cowardly Lion have
many adventures on their strange and sometimes
frightening journey.

READ MORE IN PUFFIN

For children of all ages, Puffin represents quality and variety – the very best in publishing today around the world.

For complete information about books available from Puffin – and Penguin – and how to order them, contact us at the appropriate address below. Please note that for copyright reasons the selection of books varies from country to country.

On the worldwide web: www.puffin.co.uk

In the United Kingdom: Please write to *Dept. EP, Penguin Books Ltd, Bath Road, Harmondsworth, West Drayton, Middlesex UB7 0DA*
Schools Line in the UK: Please write to

In the United States: Please write to *Consumer Sales, Penguin USA, P.O. Box 999, Dept. 17109, Bergenfield, New Jersey 07621-0120*. VISA and MasterCard holders call 1-800-253-6476 to order Penguin titles

In Canada: Please write to *Penguin Books Canada Ltd, 10 Alcorn Avenue, Suite 300, Toronto, Ontario M4V 3B2*

In Australia: Please write to *Penguin Books Australia Ltd, P.O. Box 257, Ringwood, Victoria 3134*

In New Zealand: Please write to *Penguin Books (NZ) Ltd, Private Bag 102902, North Shore Mail Centre, Auckland 10*

In India: Please write to *Penguin Books India Pvt Ltd, 706 Eros Apartments, 56 Nehru Place, New Delhi 110 019*

In the Netherlands: Please write to *Penguin Books Netherlands bv, Postbus 3507, NL-1001 AH Amsterdam*

In Germany: Please write to *Penguin Books Deutschland GmbH, Metzlerstrasse 26, 60594 Frankfurt am Main*

In Spain: Please write to *Penguin Books S. A., Bravo Murillo 19, 1° B, 28015 Madrid*

In Italy: Please write to *Penguin Italia s.r.l., Via Felice Casati 20, I–20124 Milano*

In France: Please write to *Penguin France S. A., 17 rue Lejeune, F–31000 Toulouse*

In Japan: Please write to *Penguin Books Japan, Ishikiribashi Building, 2–5–4, Suido, Bunkyo-ku, Tokyo 112*

In South Africa: Please write to *Longman Penguin Southern Africa (Pty) Ltd, Private Bag X08, Bertsham 2013*